CLAIMED BY THE ELVEN BROTHERS: FATE

AN ELVEN KING NOVELLA #2

CRISTINA RAYNE

http://CristinaRayneAuthor.blogspot.com

ISBN-10: 0692297871
ISBN-13: 978-0692297872 (Paperback)

Dedicated to all my readers who are always willing to come along for the ride—no matter how convoluted

Also by Cristina Rayne

Claimed by the Elven King
Claimed by the Elven Brothers: Decision (An Elven King Novella #1)
Blood Escort: A Short Story (Erotic Tales from the Vampire Underground) #1

Urban and Epic Fantasy writing as C.G. Garcia

The Supreme Moment (A Fractured Multiverse Novel)
Black Crimson (Blood Fire Chronicles Book 1)
(A Fractured Multiverse Novel) *coming Fall 2014

Old Souls (Book 1)
The Ties That Bind the Soul (Old Souls Book 2)
Old Souls Book 3 *coming Fall 2014

CHAPTER ONE

I was so nervous that I was actually starting to feel really queasy.

Seren lounged beside me, talking about who-knows-what as I had unconsciously started to tune him out while I stared hard into the hazy distance for signs of movement. Locien had been gone for quite some time, but with time flowing differently in the Inbetween, I had no way of knowing if only ten minutes had passed within the elven realm or an hour.

After everything they and Emily had told me about the elven king, I think it would have been more accurate to say that I was terrified to meet him rather than nervous. I couldn't even imagine what a man that had lived over two thousand years would be like, not to mention one who physically radiated power.

That thought brought me up short, and I turned to Seren. "I can't believe I never asked either of you this, but how old are you two exactly?"

Seren blinked at me curiously. "What brought such a question on so suddenly?"

"I was just thinking about the impossibility of the elven king's age and realized I had never asked."

"Would it bother you were we both His Majesty's age?" he asked.

"Bother...I don't think so. More like let me put several things in perspective. The way all of you have described your king makes him seem like something that couldn't possibly exist outside of a story—more than elves, I mean. To actually *meet* someone like that face-to-face..." I shivered. "I guess what I'm trying to say is that it wouldn't be so overwhelming if it turns out I had already met a couple of elves just as old and who aren't so—sorry—*alien*." I smiled a little embarrassedly.

"I see."

As Seren studied me with a thoughtful expression, I got the feeling that he didn't quite believe me. It made me wonder if he had seen something in my expression that I hadn't intended.

"Well? Are you going to tell me or not?" I demanded when the silence stretched on longer than was comfortable.

"Only if you are certain…" he hedged.

"Even if you say you're ten thousand years old I'm not going to freak out," I said, rolling my eyes. "In fact, it would be really interesting. I bet you would have quite the fascinating stories to tell because I refuse to believe someone could've lived that long without at least a *couple* of exciting things happening to them. That would be too depressing."

He smiled prettily, and my mind seemed to lose focus for a few seconds as I found myself unable to look away from his mouth. "Quite a few, yes, although not nearly ten thousand years' worth. His Majesty is several centuries older than either of us. Locien is a bit over fifteen hundred years old, and I am three years shy of twelve hundred."

"Somehow—I thought you were going to say something like two or three hundred." I shook my head incredulously. "That you two are brothers born three hundred years apart is even more mindboggling. I must seem awfully young to you."

"You are a human, so there can be no comparison," he said. "Just as it does within the Inbetween, time flows differently for our two races."

"Yeah. Emily said pretty much the same thing to me, that it was hard for her to get used to an elf's sense of time in the beginning."

"Something my brother and I would do well to

remember," he said with a nod before his eyes suddenly flickered out towards the meadow before us.

I immediately whipped my head towards the meadow as well, my back suddenly so stiff with tension that I'm surprised it didn't creak. Sure enough, four figures were emerging from the distant gloom, and that was the cue for my throat to tighten with tension as well, so much that I was having trouble swallowing against the huge lump that had formed in my throat.

I stared hard at all four as they neared, my eyes instantly latching on to the couple walking a few steps ahead of the other two. One, I was relieved to see was Emily, but the elf beside her, a platinum blond man with hair just as long as hers, had every instinct within my body crying out for me to get my ass off the ground and *run*!

So of course I froze and gaped at them like an idiot.

Even from that distance I could see that he was glowing a brilliant, yellow light. I winced and jerked my eyes away as if I had accidently looked directly at the sun through a break in the clouds but not soon enough to prevent me from seeing spots. It looked as though walking so close to him should have burned, or at the very least, been uncomfortable for Emily, but not only was the Royal Wife holding his hand, but the light didn't seem to bother her at all even as it illuminated her as well.

I jumped as I felt Seren place his hand on my shoulder. "Come. Let us stand to greet them," he urged.

I never took my eyes off the couple—well, Emily at least—as I climbed onto shaky legs. I grimaced. How embarrassing would it be to meet the king of the elves while obviously trembling like a frightened kid…

"Bow to His Majesty once they are nearly upon us," Seren murmured, causing me to look over at him sharply. Damn, but I was going to have to learn all that courtly crap now wasn't I? As though reading my mind, he suddenly grinned and added, "It is only polite."

Rather than say something snarky, I merely nodded with a sharp jerk of my head. Well, at least he hadn't asked me to curtsey. There was no way I would have been able to do it right, and the last thing I wanted to do was look stupid here no matter how nice and benign the elven king supposedly was.

When they were only a couple of yards away, Seren bowed, and I hastily followed his lead. As I lifted my eyes, I instantly had to look away from the king's eye-watering figure and focus my gaze on Emily, instead. I returned her friendly smile as Locien walked around her to come stand by my side while the unknown elf accompanying him stopped to stand about an arms-length behind the royal couple.

Then Emily stepped closer to the king until the side of her body was pressed against his, and as if a light switch had been flipped off, the brilliant glow in my peripheral view disappeared. I couldn't resist turning my gaze curiously to the elven king's face.

He looks almost human, was my first, surprised thought.

However, a second, more scrutinizing look quickly had me thinking differently. Although his face was a bit wider than every other elf I had met so far, that was where the similarities to a human man ended. The ridiculously smooth and perfect skin beneath the intricate silver crown of vines at his brow could never belong to a human.

His eerie green eyes immediately fixed on me, and something primal within my brain shriveled up and screamed in terror. Only being sandwiched between Seren and Locien, Seren's hand resting against my back in support, stopped me from acting on my very real urge to run away.

They were right. Just one look and I was ready to collapse onto my knees. I could feel his presence like a heavy film in the air weighing down onto every inch of my body, making it harder to breathe. How in the world could Emily handle being so near to him, hell, to have him look at her with such intense eyes, especially when the two of them—images of last night's lovemaking with the brothers abruptly flooded my mind. I hastily clamped down on that line of thinking. What the hell was *wrong* with me? Now was *not* the time for my mind to be in the gutter!

My heart was beating so frantically that my chest had begun to hurt, the pounding resounding so loudly in my ears that I was sure that everyone else could hear it. I took a deep breath and forced myself to calm down, to meet the elven king's gaze with as benign an expression as I could manage.

"I am King Sethian of the Royal House of Elerren," he said, his tone conversational and nowhere near the booming, powerful voice I had expected.

I felt myself relax minutely. "Megan Reyes. It's nice to meet you," I managed to reply without too much trouble considering my throat was still tight and my mouth dry with anxiety.

He nodded. "My cousin has informed me that you have accepted their proposal to enter the House of Elerren as a mistress until such a time that a child is born and a husband named."

"I have," I said, relieved that my voice didn't sound as strained this time.

"You understand," the elven king continued, "that you will be physically altered in order to enter our realm, that you will no longer have any contact with the human realm from this point on?"

"Yes."

Putting it so bluntly, it made me wonder how many women might have backed out after hearing it when they realized that this really was the point of no return. I hadn't paused at all in my answer, but having the reality of leaving the life I had built and my friends behind forever had briefly made my anxiety level shoot through the roof. I knew I probably should have thought this through a *lot* more, but I had always been an impulsive person, often to my detriment. Hopefully this time I wouldn't regret jumping into something so hastily.

For a long, uncomfortable moment, the king studied me, and it was hard not to look away, especially when it seemed those piercing eyes could see all the way down to the depths of my soul. Then he finally gave a curt nod and raised a hand.

"Come forth, Megan," he beckoned simply.

I glanced at Emily, who smiled and nodded ever so slightly in reassurance. Even still, when I stepped towards King Sethian, my movements were stilted and cautious. I had no idea what this powerful creature was about to do, and it was scary no matter how many times I told myself that he wasn't here to hurt me.

Once only about a foot separated us, he placed his raised hand onto my forehead, making every alarm bell in my mind go off, but I forced myself not to flinch away, staring at his face with what I was sure was wide eyes. This close and I could literally feel the energy coming off his body, the air vibrating as though I was standing too close to a rather large, exposed live wire.

However, his touch was surprisingly cool, and as he continued to stare down into my eyes, it didn't feel as though he was doing anything to me at all. Even so, I couldn't relax to save my life.

Only when my chest began to burn did I realize that I had literally stopped breathing, and I drew in a shaky breath just as he lowered his hand from my forehead. The elven king smiled and something deep within my psyche seemed to loosen.

He then looked at both Seren and Locien briefly in turn and said in a rather formal voice, "Your petition is granted." He turned his attention back to me and continued in a warmer tone, "I welcome you, Megan, to the elven realm and to my family."

"Thanks," I replied and immediately cringed at the utter casualness of my response.

I belatedly added a bow to my reply, but King

Sethian looked more amused than anything and nodded his head slightly in acceptance. He beckoned forward the thus far silent elf that had accompanied them.

"Glanthal is a mage of the House of Elerren. He will now change your body so that you may enter into our realm."

I nodded as I eyed Glanthal a bit nervously. Just how much of me was he going to change right now?

"Don't worry," Emily said, drawing my attention. Her smile was sympathetic. "You'll only feel something like a cold wave wash through you. It'll be a little uncomfortable at first, but not painful. Just concentrate on breathing slowly and deeply, and you'll be fine."

Not painful this time, *you mean*, I thought with an inward grimace. Seren had been fairly blunt about how much being changed would hurt when he had tried to explain the process to me earlier. I *really* didn't want to think about that right now.

"When you lose your sight, I shall lead you," Seren added. "Glanthal will complete the process once we are within the Realm."

"Okay—I'm ready," I said as steadily as I could.

I stood absolutely still as Glanthal reached over to encircle both my upper arms in a firm grip. I instantly felt an overwhelming urge to close my eyes tightly, but I stubbornly fixed my gaze on the mage-elf's face, wondering what, if anything, I would see of the process.

Just as Emily had warned, the elf's previously lukewarm hands suddenly chilled, and before I could blink, something like an icy gust of wind entered my body from his hands and began to spread out. I gasped sharply as the sudden cold was just shy of painful, but I didn't dare move—even when my vision winked out as though someone had turned off a huge, cosmic light switch.

Almost immediately, I felt someone take my hand—probably Seren—and I couldn't help clutching at it tightly even though I hadn't wanted any of them to know just how scared I was at that moment.

They will fix this. The blindness is only temporary, so get a grip!

"Are you all right, Megan?" Seren asked, giving my hand a reassuring squeeze.

"Yeah," I answered simply, not wanting to risk my voice shaking.

"Remember," Emily suddenly spoke up, "once the transmutation's been performed and you're settled, come see me."

"I will," I replied towards the general direction of her voice.

"Come," Seren said, tugging my hand gently forward. "Let us bring you to your new home."

CHAPTER TWO

I hadn't expected to scream—hell, to even *cry*— but I did. It was a good thing that my imagination regarding the level of pain had failed me quite spectacularly or else I likely would never have had the guts to go through with the change. It felt as though Glanthal had dipped my entire body into a vat of acid, and I was feeling my skin and muscles melt away piece by piece.

I screamed and screamed and still the pain seemed to impossibly increase until the whole terrible episode began to seem surreal, as though it was someone else screaming and someone else writhing in agony. I was either on the verge of passing out or my mind was about to break, and at that point, I would have welcomed either as long as the pain stopped.

Then from one scream to the next, the worst of the pain abruptly vanished, leaving behind only echoes of torment and the sound of my sobs. I could now feel myself digging my nails into what was probably someone's forearm as I clutched at it tightly. Someone was talking to me, their voice sounding as far away and faint as though they were speaking across the vast expanse of a canyon, and I couldn't make out any of the words. The roaring of my own blood in my ears and the sobs I just couldn't seem to stop easily drowned out everything else.

I tried to tune everything out as I concentrated on pulling myself together, trying to slow my rapid, shuddering breaths to something a bit less noisy. More voices began filtering into my awareness, but they were still nothing more than a cacophony of sounds to my traumatized mind. Hands also began touching my arms, my forehead, and my legs, and after the first couple of times, I tried not to flinch. It was probably just Seren and Locien trying to comfort me.

It was over.

I had survived the horrendous pain, a pain I would never have to go through again. That thought, along with the rapidly fading vestiges of pain, were what finally allowed me to calm both my breathing and my mind.

Slowly, I released my death-grip on the unknown arm and began wiping the tears from my eyes, suddenly feeling painfully embarrassed that I had actually full-out cried. I grimaced. What a great first impression I was making on everyone.

"Megan?"

I turned my head towards the voice, recognizing it as Seren's.

"I'm okay now, right?" I couldn't help but ask plaintively. God, but my voice sounded as if I had swallowed a dozen razor blades.

A warm hand gently cupped my cheek. "It's done," Seren replied.

"You may take her home now," Glanthal said. "Although I do not believe it will take so long, call me at once if her vision has not returned by tomorrow."

The rest of their conversation was lost to me as both the mage and everyone else shifted to speaking in the elven language. I felt a mild twinge of irritation as it felt as though they were talking about me behind my back, but I was just too tired to feel any real anger.

I blindly reached out a hand and grabbed at whom I assumed was Seren. "Will you help me sit up?"

I had expected to feel queasy, but other than a

little weakness, I felt fine once I was upright. I swung my legs over the edge of the marble table. I had actually felt a tinge of fear when Seren had first set me down onto it and had urged me to lie down flat onto my back. Visions of stone altars and maiden sacrifices had flowed through my head before I had given myself a mental slap on the head for even thinking something so ridiculous.

"Do you think you can walk?" The voice was Locien's this time.

"One way to find out," I said with a weak smile as I slowly pushed myself off the edge until my bare feet touched the cold, smooth floor.

Hands immediately grabbed at one of my elbows, but other than a little shakiness, my legs held up just fine. My smile became a little more genuine.

"I'm good."

"Then let us take you home," Seren said eagerly.

Not being able to see was an experience I hoped to never have to repeat.

Even now, as I sat on a couch of some sort sandwiched between Seren and Locien, I couldn't help running a hand over my other arm again and again just to make sure the skin was still there and not the bare bone I half-feared. I really hoped that my sight wouldn't take all day to come back. Whether I wanted to admit it or not, I was dying to see what changes had been made to me. I still felt a little discomfited about the idea of me looking so much like an elf now.

I was also really anxious to see my new home. The descriptions that Seren had given me just didn't cut it. I couldn't help but imagine some kind of fairy-tale castle on a hill, but as this particular castle was centuries old, the reality would probably be far from that pristine image. Unless they used magic, the building, itself, would likely be riddled with cracks or look as weathered as the ancient buildings in my world.

Locien was currently telling me a bit about the family members—cousins as their parents were both deceased—that I would be meeting as soon as my eyesight had returned and I'd had a chance to explore and settle myself within the wing of the royal palace the brothers shared. It was almost surreal to think that I would be living in something as grandiose as a palace now.

Just thinking about all the things I wanted to see made me doubly impatient for my brain to get over the trauma of the change enough for my vision to come back. I wondered how long it had taken Emily to regain her sight. It had never occurred to me to ask her back when we'd still been within the Inbetween, and I was kicking myself about it now.

Maybe what I needed was as simple as a good, long nap.

I blindly reached over and touched what I hoped was Locien's leg, causing him to break off in midword.

"I think I should go lay down for now," I said before either one could say a word.

"Are you still in pain?" Seren asked with concern.

I quickly shook my head. "Not even a little bit. I'm just really eager for my sight to come back and thought maybe it'd come back quicker if I slept a little."

The cushion beside me shifted, and I suddenly found myself being gathered into somebody's arms. I clumsily grabbed onto the other's shoulders, unable to tell by feel and smell alone which of the two held me. One night of fantastic sex was hardly enough time for that level of familiarity.

"I could've walked," I said with a chuckle.

"Yes," Seren replied simply right into my ear, answering my question of who was carrying me.

"I'm sorry that you two are stuck babysitting me today. I should've asked Emily how long it took her to get her eyesight back."

"Glanthal did say that your blindness could last a day or two and that everyone was different, so knowing whether it had taken the Royal Wife a mark or ten days to regain her sight would not have mattered at all," Locien pointed out.

"Besides," Seren added, "assuring you have an easy transition into the elven realm and our household is the least we can do after asking so much from you."

I shrugged, feeling embarrassed suddenly. By coming here, I had given up a lot less than he was thinking. The only thing I would miss from my world was my friends. My grandmother had been the only family I'd had, and my friends had somewhat filled the void in my heart her death had left behind. Yet, I knew that their friendship would never be enough. I desperately needed that extra *something*, something that I might just find here living with these two incredible men.

At least, that was my hope.

CHAPTER THREE

When I groggily cracked my eyes opened, the first thing I did was turn my head to look at the clock on my nightstand. Instead of bright red digits, I was greeted by the somewhat blurry sight of impossibly smooth, pale hands holding a thick book opened over someone's lap. My eyes instantly flew open the rest of the way, and I shot upright, startling the owner of said hands.

"Megan?" Seren asked worriedly, rising from the velvet-draped chair beside my bed and moving to sit on the edge of the bed at my feet.

I laughed and ran a hand over my face. "I'm okay. I just forgot where I was for a second there."

Seren's concerned frown relaxed into an easy smile, and only then, as I stared at his mouth in sudden fascination, did I realize that I was actually *seeing* his mouth quite clearly.

"I can see again!" I exclaimed ecstatically. "*Finally*!"

I immediately began looking around the room. It was much larger than I had expected, easily larger than my entire apartment back in my world. The bed was located in the exact center of the room, bookended by a couple of nightstands. I was a bit bummed to see that there weren't any windows, but there were plenty of lamps—oil lamps I realized in surprise on closer scrutiny—one on each nightstand and two more across the room sitting on the surface of what looked like a wooden vanity. They illuminated the room well in a bright yellow/orange glow, making the room feel more open and less stuffy than it should.

There were also three doors, and I immediately had the urge to go exploring. I was such a terrible snoop by nature. It was no wonder that I hadn't been able to resist going back over and over again to the brothers' "doorway."

However, exploring would have to wait just a little longer. There was something much more important I had to do first.

"Do you have a mirror somewhere around here?" I asked as I moved to swing my legs over the side of the bed.

Seren instantly reached over and stilled my movements with a hand against my chest before I could start to rise.

"I'll bring one," he offered as he stood and walked over to the vanity I had spied earlier.

He quickly returned with one of those old-fashioned oval hand mirrors you often saw in period movies. This one was a lovely bronze color. He seemed to hesitate a bit as he handed it to me, and I wondered if he was afraid that I would freak out. I was suddenly nervous. Did I look *that* much different?

I took a deep breath and brought the mirror up to eye level, gripping the long, smooth handle tightly.

My first thought was, *That can't be me.*

I mean, the pale woman staring back at me looked so—fake. No, doll-like, like one of those delicate porcelain dolls in an antique shop. My skin was much too smooth and unblemished to be real.

I raised a hand to my cheek and gently pressed my index finger into it, half-afraid that my skin would feel as smooth and hard as the mirror in my hand, but the butter-soft skin easily dented with even such a tentative pressure, to my extreme relief.

Even though I had expected it—or been *warned* was the better term—it was still a shock to see a pair of leaf-green eyes staring back with a somewhat dazed look. Was I really making such a stupid face?

However, despite all the changes, I could still see myself. The foundation was still very much there, just polished up a bit and given a new, different coat of paint. I was different but still very much the same, and like Emily, there were no new pointed ears.

I was still very much human—at least for now, remembering the uncanny way Emily had moved.

As I lowered the mirror, the grin I directed at Seren was actually genuine. "Everyone made such a big deal about my transmutation that I didn't expect to recognize myself at all," I confessed.

Seren had been silently watching me with a slight tension in his demeanor, but whatever he saw in my expression allowed that tension to melt away. He grinned back at me in turn.

"Some of the brides were quite upset after seeing themselves after the change," he said.

I nodded. "It *is* really shocking at first, but I'll get used to it. It's not like I spend all that much time looking in mirrors, anyway. The important thing for me is that I don't really *feel* all that different."

I stretched slowly. "Did I sleep long?"

"Just a couple of marks at the most."

"Marks?" I asked, tilting my head quizzically.

"A lesser measurement of time within the elven realm," he explained. "It's equivalent to about a human hour and a half."

"I guess Locien had to leave? There really was no sense in both of you staying with me while I slept."

"This is a very delicate time," Seren said. "We thought it best that he spend time with Hilde while you slept."

"Oh—right—of course," I stammered uncomfortably.

The three-ton bright pink elephant in the room had suddenly made itself known.

"I know you said that the wives are kept out of sight of each other, but will I ever meet her?" I asked carefully.

"If that is what you wish," he replied just as carefully, his gaze suddenly scrutinizing. "Hilde very much wishes to meet you—but perhaps not for a while, if only for your sake."

"*Mine?*" I echoed incredulously.

Seren nodded. "As I explained before, the promise of a child can change one's perspective on several things."

"Then—someday I'd like to meet her, too," I said softly, more than guilt making my chest tighten painfully.

It reminded me that I really had jumped into this way too prematurely—or maybe "stupidly," "recklessly" were better words to describe my actions.

Seren abruptly reached over and took me into his arms, hugging me gently. "Forgive me," he said. "That discussion should not have occurred today."

"No—it's okay. It is what it is, and pretending the situation doesn't exist will do none of us any good here."

"Nevertheless, we shall not discuss it any further today."

I closed my eyes within his warm embrace and nodded.

Yes, "stupidly" was definitely the correct word.

CHAPTER FOUR

The prospect of being presented to all the head honchos of the House of Elerren made me feel as though I was about to undergo a particularly nerve-wracking job interview that I absolutely had to ace. Although they were all only cousins to Seren and Locien, some of them were much older than the brothers, and according to Seren, often wanted to treat them as children rather than the deference their titles as Stewards of the House of Elerren mandated.

Politics was not something I had ever given much, if any, thought to, and to suddenly be thrust neck deep within the worst kind intimidated the hell out of me. Discrimination I knew how to handle, and I've never had any problems with socializing. However, I had never been any good with the types of social *games* the wealthy always seemed to play, never mind understand their convoluted rules. Now here I was expected to play those same games within a culture that was completely alien to me. No doubt I would commit several social *faux pas* before everything was said and done.

The best I could hope for was to not embarrass all of us *too* much.

As I walked between Seren and Locien towards their household's main parlor, I suddenly had a powerful urge to grab both men's hands for a little physical support. Only the thought of how ridiculous we would look as we entered a room where all eyes would be on us—like parents holding the hands of an unruly child—kept my hands firmly at my sides.

I was also feeling slightly uncomfortable in the unfamiliar style of the dress the House's maids or servants or whatever they were called had helped lace me into. Needless to say, I had never worn anything resembling a true corset and was not at all enjoying the sensation of slowly being squeezed to death.

At least the two elven women had been friendly and rather chatty. They had seemed genuinely excited that Seren and Locien had finally found their potential bride. I cringed to think how awkward it would have been had they been part of the anti-human crowd.

When we paused outside what I assumed was

the double doors to the parlor, I felt myself stiffen so much in anxiety that I would have given an iron pole a run for its money. Not for the first time today, I wondered why I had ever thought this whole adventure would be a good idea.

"Relax," Locien said abruptly, making me jump.

I turned to him and gave him what was probably a half-assed smile.

"This is simply a formality," he continued. "You need not speak at all if that is what you wish. Seren and I shall take care of everything."

I could feel some of the tension in my shoulders ease as I nodded in relief. "Good, because I would have no clue what to say. I've never had to do anything so—formal before." *...or been on display...*

Seren reached over and squeezed my shoulder in a gesture of comfort as Locien opened the doors and waved us through. The first impression I got of the room was that it was open and spacious, like the lobby of a large hotel. *Make that a super expensive hotel,* I amended as my eyes quickly took in the various ornate furnishings scattered along the walls and clustered in the center.

It was there in the center that a group of elves were seated in two different groups, watching us enter the room, some with open curiosity, but most with narrowed, keen eyes. As Seren steered me over to the more severe-looking group, I immediately had the urge to fidget, but through sheer force of will, I managed to keep myself stiff and my hands loose and casual at my sides.

We stopped a couple of feet from them, Seren and Locien taking a position on either side of me. Trying not to be obvious about it, I did a quick sweep of the group. There were seven elves total, five men and two women. They all looked to be the same age, late twenties-early thirties, but by now, I knew better. Since these people were the elders of the royal family, they had to at least be several thousand years old given their life-spans and the ages of my two suitors.

It was Locien that spoke first. "My lords and ladies, may I present Megan, our newest member and bride-to-be. Megan, these are the elders of the House of Elerrin."

He pointed to the man standing on the far left and began to name everyone. I glanced at each in turn and nodded a greeting, but their names were so unfamiliar that I doubted I would be able to remember them, let alone keep everyone straight in my mind, especially when they all were staring at me stone-faced and their mouths set in, to me, what looked like thin lines of disapproval.

Or maybe they just always looked like this.

The elder I think Locien had named Galanir, a man with the most platinum blond hair this side of white I had ever seen, stood and offered me a tight smile that never quite reached his eyes. "We welcome you, Megan of the human realm. May the high powers bless your union with the Stewards of our House."

Inside, I squirmed. Was I supposed to say something? Thanks? It's good to be here? I settled for stiffly bowing my head to them. It seemed the safest choice.

As I raised my head, I felt Seren take my hand. "Come meet some of the cousins," he said when I looked at him quizzically.

So the exhibition was over. Although the experience had been relatively painless as the brothers had promised, I still felt a profound sense of relief that the spotlight would no longer be directly on me. It helped that Locien remained behind to speak with the elders, capturing all their attention for the time being.

Approaching the second group, I could tell that these elves, at least, would be a bit friendlier as none of them appeared to have the same stick shoved up their ass like their elders, and their faces were at least open and animated.

Seren led me over to one of the more open-faced seated men, who immediately rose to his feet in greeting. "Megan, this is our cousin, Teyan."

I nodded and smiled. "Nice to meet you."

"I am pleased that you have decided to join our family," Teyan said, flashing me a genuine smile. "I have yet to be granted permission to find my own secondary bride, but when I do, I would hope that you would guide her in her initial days as the Royal Wife has pledged to guide you."

I blinked in surprise at his candidness. "Of course."

"Lord Galanir is his father." Seren added, pointing at the sour-faced looking elf across the room that had "greeted" me earlier. "Those of his lineage serve as the royal treasurers."

The personalities of the father and son couldn't have been any different, though there was some resemblance as they did have the same striking shade of silver-blond hair. Where Galanir seemed all hard edges and coldness, Teyan projected something warm and calm. As a result, I felt some of my own rigidness begin to relax.

Teyan reached over and grasped Seren's forearm in what looked like an elven version of a handshake. "May you bless the House of Elerren with many sons and daughters," he said sincerely.

...*but not for a while*, I added mentally. First, I

needed time to process all these strange and over-whelming experiences, to become comfortable in this new alien culture. I needed time just to *be* before adding a baby to the mix, and according to Emily, because of the change, I now had plenty of it.

Today marked the first day of the rest of my life, and all things considering, I wasn't off to a bad start.

CHAPTER FIVE

I was surprised when the person standing behind the door was Emily, herself, rather than one of her servants, and then I was surprised that I had been surprised at all. I had only been within the elven realm for about a day, and it seemed my thoughts and expectations were already being affected. It was a bit disconcerting.

"It's good to see you again, Megan," Emily said in greeting as she gestured for me to come in.

"Thanks for having me over," I said as I entered into what looked like her living room, though on a much grander, more elegant scale than I was used to.

"Seren told me that you're usually at Court with the king around this time, so I really appreciate you taking the time to hang out with me," I added as we both sat down on one of the couches.

"Believe me, it's *you* that's doing *me* the favor," she replied with a grin. "Court is nothing more than an excuse for the nobility to argue and posture. Having to listen to that kind of nonsense gets old rather quickly. Besides, I am only there to keep Sethian's power from overwhelming everyone to the point of unconsciousness. It's probably a good thing to remind them of it every once in a while."

"No kidding," I said, remembering that strange heaviness in the air when I had met the elven king before Emily had done whatever she had done to turn that power off. "I imagine they wouldn't be so keen to argue with that kind of power doing its damndest to make them kiss the floor."

"So, how are you adjusting so far?"

"Definitely much better today. Once I got past the pain of having my body melted and remade and my eyesight came back, Seren and Locien had the great idea of introducing me to the rest of the family." I made a face. "It was like standing on a stage and suddenly realizing that you were naked. I could practically feel everyone's eyes tearing me apart."

Emily smiled sympathetically. "The elders of the family are a rather stuffy and severe bunch. Most of them are older than even Sethian, sometimes by thousands of years, and even I find it hard to relate to them after all this time."

"I got the feeling that some of them were less than stoked about the idea of me being there," I confided.

"For what it's worth, I don't think it's because you're human. Most of them have sons that are eager to find a human bride of their own."

I nodded. "Yeah, I met a couple of those. Maybe they were just, I don't know, scandalized about the threesome nature of our agreement. For all I know, elves are a bunch of prudes, and Seren and Locien are just free spirits."

Emily laughed. "No, definitely not prudes, just private. Also, you'll soon learn just how uptight everyone is about social status. That you were introduced as a *mistress* and not a bride probably was the cause of the disapproval that you sensed. However, since your patrons are the Stewards of the House of Elerren, they will never say anything to you outright."

"Thank God for small favors. Are your children away today?" I asked. "I was hoping to meet them."

The truth was, I was really curious to see what a child born to an elf and a human looked like. Would their human parentage be obvious?

"My daughters are out with two of my ladies-in-waiting for a lesson. They should be back shortly. My second oldest, Anir, is off learning mage-craft in another province, so it'll probably be a few moon-cycles before you'll get to meet him. My oldest is with his father at Court."

"No, he's not," a deep, unknown voice suddenly said directly behind me, making me nearly jump clear out of my skin.

With my heart in my throat, I whirled around to see a tall, black-haired man looking down at me with bright, emerald eyes filled with amusement—and he was the most exotic, beautiful creature I had ever seen. His hair, like a waterfall of black silk, fell to his mid-back, making me have the most absurd itch to run my fingers through it just to see if it was as soft and silky as it looked. The contrast between the pale, alabaster skin of his face and that hair was quite striking, as were the two pale elf ears that poked through his hair. Like the elven king, this young man physically radiated power, even if my eyes couldn't see it.

A huge sigh sounded beside me, and I tore my eyes away from that exquisite sight to see Emily looking over her shoulder with an exasperated expression.

"I really wish you would use the door, Thaylan," she scolded.

Thaylan...where have I heard...

My eyes widened in sudden recognition. *This* extraordinary man was Emily's *son?*

He shrugged, flashing me a grin. "You usually take your visitors to the balcony so..."

"Megan, this is my oldest son, Thaylan," Emily introduced. "Thaylan, this is Megan, your new cousin-to-be."

Thaylan smiled and held out his hand, which I took gingerly for a brief handshake. I have to admit that I was a little surprised that elves would shake hands the human way. And no matter how you looked at him, this man was one hundred percent elf. There was nothing about him that indicated that he was half human, though I did wonder how he had ended up with black hair when Emily was a brunette and his father platinum blond. Maybe all half-breeds were born with black hair? I would have to ask Emily later.

"Welcome to the family," Thaylan said.

"Thanks, and it's nice to finally meet you."

"I can't believe that the morning Court is already finished," Emily said.

"We have your absence to thank, Mom. When today's petitioners and envoys realized that they would be facing Father in his true form, suddenly all their grievances did not seem worth bringing before the king after all. We ended up adjudicated only a handful."

"You're smiling now, but I would be willing to bet that the amount of petitions will double once they see me back at your father's side."

"I shall worry about tomorrow when tomorrow comes," he said with a dismissive wave of his hand. "For now, Rinya and I have a certain project that could use a little extra attention now that I've been prematurely relieved from that daily time suck."

It was weird to hear an elf use such a human phrase. Maybe that was the only human legacy passed onto him.

"She's still at arms practice with Rinwen and Saeria," Emily informed him.

For a brief moment, the grin he flashed his mother transformed his face from a marble Adonis to a mischievous little boy that was rather jarring.

"It's been quite a while since I've had the pleasure of sparring with those two. Perhaps they will indulge me today."

Emily snorted. "They would spar with you for the next thousand years straight if you let them. Be sure to send Rinya and Arra back here for the midday meal. Megan will be visiting with me and a few other human brides until at least this evening, and I would like them to meet her as well."

Thaylan nodded, and then after giving me a nod as well, to my utter astonishment, the air around him seemed to shimmer and warp as his entire body rapidly faded out of existence like a ghost.

"What—just happened?" I asked, turning to

look at Emily in bewilderment.

"Elven magic, for lack of a better word," she replied. "Both Sethian and Thaylan have the ability to 'phase' in and out of this spatial dimension by warping the very fabric of reality. It's a very rare ability even among the elves, so those two are the only ones you'll ever likely see do it."

"So what you're saying is that the king and your son are both mages like Glanthal?" I said, struggling to understand.

She shook her head. "Only Thaylan is a mage. Sethian is—well, to be frank, neither one of them can really be classified so easily. They both have unique abilities that set them apart from everyone else, but those particular explanations are better left for after you have lived in the Realm for a while. It's all rather complicated."

I shrugged more nonchalantly than I was feeling. "It's enough just to know they can do those kinds of things rather than the hows and whys of it. I've seen more incredible things in the last twenty-four hours than I ever thought I would in my entire life. I'm not sure my brain could handle any more earth-shattering revelations right now."

"Speaking of revelations, how much have you been able to talk with Locien and Seren about the elven realm, itself?" Emily asked.

"Not nearly enough," I said with a frown. "I spent most of yesterday either blind or sleeping off the trauma of the change, and then before we could even talk about much of anything, I was being laced into a *very* uncomfortable dress and herded to a meeting with the future in-laws, so to speak. Seren did tell me this morning that he had arranged to completely spend the next couple of days with me. Apparently, tomorrow Locien has to travel to someplace called Nallos on some sort of family business and he wanted to make sure that I wouldn't be left alone so soon. He said that there was something he wanted to show me. I have to admit, I'm curious as hell about it."

"Ah," Emily said knowingly, but maddeningly, she didn't elaborate.

I considered pestering her until she told me, but in the end decided maybe it was better not to ruin the surprise. Seren had been almost giddy last night when he had told me about it.

Remembering last night, I frowned. I had totally expected us three to have sex again once we had returned to their suite after my uncomfortable presentation to the family, but after giving me a thorough tour of their wing of the palace and making sure I had everything I needed, they both had bade me goodnight at the door to the bedroom they had given me with only a parting kiss on my cheek. I hadn't expected Locien to stay the entire night with me, being married and all, but at the very least, I had hoped that Seren and I could sleep together even if there could be no sex.

I had a weakness for having a warm body wrapped around me while I slept. Missing that warmth was likely the reason why I would frequently give my exes a second chance even when I knew they were no good for me. Jenna had certainly chewed me out about it often enough.

My chest tightened at the thought of my best friend. It was still too soon for anyone to miss me, but eventually someone would find my car in the airport's long-term parking lot. I had caught a cab from the airport and had the driver drop me off at the jogging trail. I was glad that I'd had the foresight to set up the lie I had fed to Jenna before I went to see my suitors in the Inbetween for the last time. Had the brothers not decided that I would leave with them to the elven realm that day, or even if they had allowed me to go back to my apartment one last time as I had suggested, I could have easily just called a cab to come pick me up. Leaving false trails that way just might end up sparing my friends a lot of unnecessary pain. That was my hope, at least.

I had also left my purse with my wallet, keys, and

cell phone hidden in a bunch of weeds against a tree near the elves' doorway. Seren had assured me that they had closed the doorway between the trees, so there was no danger of someone, jogger or police, accidentally falling into the Inbetween should they find the purse and decide to poke around.

"Megan?"

I shook myself out of those heavy thoughts and focused my attention on this new friend beside me— no, we were *family* now, weren't we?

"Sorry, my mind wandered there for a minute," I said sheepishly.

She reached over and gave my arm a squeeze. "Remember that I'm here to listen. If something's bothering you, or you have a question, don't be afraid to ask, even if you think the subject might be off-limits. I know how lonely it can feel in the beginning, even when you are surrounded by people."

I briefly debated on sharing my concerns about the lack of anything amorous happening last night, but then decided that I was probably just making a mountain out of a molehill. The likely explanation was that they were worried about the aftereffects of the change and wanted me to rest a little more before doing something so—vigorous.

"Thanks," I said sincerely. "It's finally starting to sink in just how crazy it was to jump into all of this so quickly. Just knowing that I have someone to talk to here is a *huge* relief."

"Are you regretting coming here?" Emily asked with concern.

I shook my head. "I really do think that I can be happy here. My life was going absolutely nowhere, so I can never regret accepting the chance Seren and Locien have given me. I just hope that I won't screw everything up. I don't exactly have the best track record when it comes to relationships, and Seren and Locien, they're so—and after seeing your beautiful son—I just don't want to screw up with them."

"Just enjoy each day as they come, and you'll be fine," Emily said firmly. "Your future is now a vast open plain as far as the eye can see rather than the single, dead-end road you feared." She abruptly rose to her feet. "Now, come. My friend, Lariel, should be here any moment now with the rest of the girls I wanted to introduce you to, so let's go wait for them out on the balcony. The view of the sea is spectacular!"

A vast plain, huh… Rather than be reassuring as she had obviously intended, the imagery made what was before me seem even more daunting. In essence, I was starting my whole life over from scratch. I could only pray that I was up to the task. After all, this time around, it wasn't just one life I had the potential to screw up.

It was four.

CHAPTER SIX

"Are you taking me on a hike or something?" I asked teasingly as I allowed Seren to lead me by the hand across one of the palace's pleasure gardens.

When we had first stepped outside, I had been expecting a completely unrecognizable, alien landscape. Instead, I was greeted by the sight of familiar-looking trees very similar to maples in the color of the trunks and the size and shapes of their leaves. Even the flowers in their various violets, pinks, and reds didn't scream "other-worldly," though their shapes were different enough that I also couldn't really name them.

The scent of nature had almost been overwhelming in the beginning so that I'd had to grab onto Seren's arm when my head had begun to swim with what was seemingly a thousand different scents. It had been like walking into one of those lotion and soap stores in the mall that inundated your nose with every scent imaginable, only times a thousand. Thankfully my head had stopped spinning after just standing completely still and slowly breathing in and out with my eyes closed for a few minutes until I had gotten used to the strong smells.

"Or something," Seren agreed, looking down at me in amusement.

"Good because I don't think I'm exactly dressed for a long walk through nature," I said, fingering the long, thin skirt of my dress in emphasis. The material was so fine that I was sure it would rip on even a blade of grass. "Are you sure you won't give me just a little hint?"

"I suppose." He pointed up ahead and to my left with his free hand. "Look there. That is our destination."

My eyes followed his hand and peered through the trees far ahead to the grassy hills beyond to see a large, rectangular building the size of an airport hanger that was built out of the same type of stones as the palace. It could have been anything from a warehouse to a hundred-car garage had the elves actually driven cars.

"I think you just made my curiosity worse," I

said with a laugh.

"I find your curiosity refreshing," Seren said. "After a thousand years of living, you begin to see less and less of it from the people around you."

"You sound so sad," I remarked uncertainly.

He flashed me his gentle smile. "It can be, but now that you and the other human brides have come here, I expect things will become lively once again. Just the princes and princesses, alone, have revitalized the court."

"Yeah, new blood always makes things more interesting," I said, thinking of the rather charming teen sisters I had met yesterday.

Emily's daughters had been full of questions about the human world, and in the process of answering them, I had realized that my old world really wasn't as dull as I had made it out to be. It was only the life that I had been living that was dull.

As we neared the mysterious building, I was surprised, then delighted to hear sounds that I was *very* familiar with, sounds that brought to mind afternoons spent with my grandmother when I was a little girl.

"It's a stable!" I blurted, ecstatic.

Suddenly it was me and not him that was tugging us forward as I increased my pace to a fast walk. I supposed I had told him about how much I had loved the horses I had grown up around on the ranch where my grandmother had worked, though the memory of that conversation had likely been among the many I had lost just because some asshole elf had played around with my brain to get back at Seren and Locien. I would have to remember to ask Seren about it later.

I rounded the corner of the building and immediately stopped dead in my tracks. Grazing in the ankle-high grass in front of the building were five of the most beautiful, yet eerie creatures I had ever seen. I had expected to see some brown palfreys, maybe a white or midnight steed, hell this was the elven realm, so maybe even a unicorn, but I never would have imagined anything like what I was currently seeing.

"What—*are* they?" I asked in something like awe.

"They are Elvensteed," Seren replied, releasing my hand to approach the nearest animal.

I watched mutely as he reached a hand to a body that was just shy of see-through and began to stroke along the side of the creature's elegant neck.

"Come," he beckoned. "They are quite tame and rather like to be stroked."

I was almost afraid to touch the steed, as if the lightest of pressures would shatter him into a million pieces like the delicate glass figurine he resembled.

However, what his nose felt like wasn't smooth and cool like blown glass but soft and warm like the finest silk. It was nothing like the sensation of stroking a regular horse's coat. It was something that made my brain stand up and take notice because the sensation did not at all match what my eyes were seeing.

"They almost look like ghosts," I said in awe. "Are you sure they're completely in our world?"

Seren laughed. "I assure you, they are quite solid. After all, they were once creatures of the human realm."

"Uh—unless you elves stole every last one of them from my world, I find that hard to believe."

He shook his head. "What you see now is centuries of transmutation of a horse from your realm."

"I—see," I replied.

Was there anything the elves *didn't* tinker with? I mean, I suppose I should've been grateful that their mages had had so much practice changing *living* things before they had gotten to *me*, but it still bothered me finding out that mucking around with something's natural form wasn't as rare as I had first assumed.

"Would you like to go for a ride with me?" Seren suddenly asked, drawing me out of my dark thoughts.

"You'd actually let me ride one?" I said excitedly.

"With me, yes," he amended, smiling at my obvious enthusiasm.

"I grew up on a ranch, you know," I said. "I know how to ride a horse."

"Yes, but these are elvensteed," he explained patiently. "They are controlled by words, not the pull of a bit and a pair of reins, and they only understand the elven language."

"Then I guess I'll have to try really hard to learn your impossible language," I grumbled, suddenly wondering if this proclamation was one of the main reasons for bringing me out here. Nothing like dangling a prize this big in front of me to give me the proper incentive.

"You will have countless years to learn my language, so do not feel as though it must be accomplished soon," he assured me. "We are all fluent in various human tongues, so you will have no problems with communication."

"Good because it'll probably take me a hundred years."

Seren turned back to the elvensteed and spoke a few phrases in his musical language. The creature immediately lowered itself to the ground.

"Climb on," Seren urged, gesturing to the strangely contoured saddle. "I shall ride behind you."

I carefully swung my leg over the saddle and sat down gingerly as far forward on the soft leather-like material as I could. Seren immediately followed, wrapping his arms around my waist and pulling me back snug against his chest. Once I was settled comfortably against his enveloping warmth, he spoke a few more elven words. The steed rose gracefully without so much as a hint of a wobble and began trotting towards the edge of the palace grounds where the hilly grasslands continued as far as the eye could see. Somehow, I thought there would be more forests in the elven realm, reminding me of how much I still had to learn about my new home.

It felt weird to be riding a horse without having any reigns clutched in my fists. I wasn't sure if I should grasp a handful of the elvensteed's semi-transparent mane or Seren's arms around me. Deciding to err on the side of caution, I covered Seren's arms with my own and gripped his wrists firmly.

Seren's arms tightened. "I shall not let you fall," he said into my ear, making the hairs on the back of my neck stand on end.

"I wasn't worried about that," I said. "I just didn't know what to do with my hands. I'm used to tugging on reigns when I ride and the saddle doesn't have anything like a pommel…"

"The saddles are designed to compliment an elvensteed's speed and movements even as it works to keep the rider from slipping off. The steed can reach speeds comparable with the fastest of your world's automobiles, and even then, provided one does not do something foolish, it is difficult to actually lose your seat."

"Really? They can go *that* fast?" I said with keen interest.

He laughed, sounding utterly delighted. "Would you like to see for yourself?"

"Of course!"

"Just hold onto my arms tightly and bend your body lower towards the steed's neck, and leave the rest to me and our companion."

I felt Seren lean with me as he spoke three Elvish words loudly. A flicker of the elvensteed's ears was the only warning before the mount suddenly shot forward as though he had been fired from a cannon. I instantly closed my eyes as the air sliced across my face and let out a shout of delight as my stomach felt as if I had left it behind, and a surge of adrenaline flooded my body. We were like the speeding train of a rollercoaster, and the natural hills of the countryside our track. Each time we crested a hill and began our decent I swore both Seren and I floated about a foot off the saddle.

By the time we slowed and I was able to open my eyes again, I was very nearly drunk on my excitement. Minus the earth-shattering sex I had experienced with the brothers, I couldn't remember the last time I had ever felt so alive. I had always loved riding horses, but there was simply no comparison to the ride I had just experienced.

Seren commanded the elvensteed again with those beautiful, flowing words, and it continued to slow until we were at only a trot.

I brushed away a strand of wayward hair that had blown across my face, and then half-turned in Seren's arms until I could see his face. His cheeks were flushed an attractive shade of rose, and his eyes were like twin emeralds as they looked back at me wide and shining with obvious joy.

"You certainly know how to show a girl a good time," I said with a wide grin. "I don't remember, but I *must* have told you how much I had loved to ride horses when I was a little girl."

"You did," he replied, his eyes betraying a slight guilt for a split-second, likely remembering that they still hadn't identified the culprit who had wiped my mind. "You seemed so excited when Locien and I described the elvensteed to you that I knew I had to show them to you right away. Not many share my love of riding just for the sake of riding, especially the play we just indulged in."

"Just say the word, and I'll go riding with you anytime," I said eagerly. Then I added a bit more hesitantly, "I don't suppose I can help take care of them? Grooming and things like that?"

He tilted his head curiously. "If that is what you wish, though some of the courtiers may wonder if you are being punished."

"Are brides not…" I made a face, "…*allowed* to do things like that?"

"It's nothing like that. Caring for beasts is just seen as work for those who aspire to a certain trade, along the lines of merchants or farmers. As one who will one day marry into the royal House of Elerren, it will seem a little odd."

I snorted. "In other words, it's a class thing. If anyone asks, you can just tell them it's one of my human quirks, that I consider it a hobby because it really would be a hobby to me. Emily and some of the other brides enjoy poking around the palace's historical archives, but I've always been more of an outdoors kind of girl. I think I would go a little crazy if I had to stay inside all the time." I suddenly smirked. "Besides, people are probably already looking at me sideways for our unconventional relationship, and every royal family has one or two eccentrics shaking things up, don't they?"

"Especially this one," Seren agreed with a chuckle. "Prince Thaylan alone ensures that things do not remain too boring within the Court for long."

"I believe it," I said, remembering his mischievous, devil-may-care smile and Emily's answering exasperation of the long-suffering.

"Ask the prince to show you his pocket dimensions sometime. They are quite a wonder to behold and an even larger wonder to experience."

"Pocket dimensions?" I echoed.

"I do not know how much the Royal Wife has told you about her son, but Prince Thaylan is quite the unique mage. He is only one of two known *Sidhe* in our long history that was born with an innate ability to create or carve out entirely new spatial dimensions using the very fabric of reality. He has been in the process of creating an entire new plane of existence since he was a young boy."

"He did say something about a 'project' when I met him yesterday..." I said faintly, completely dumbfounded by what I was hearing. Something like creating new worlds was in the realm of the gods, not something done by a person I had just shaken hands with yesterday. "I'm suddenly finding that I didn't ask *near* enough questions back when we were in the Inbetween. It seems every two seconds someone manages to pull the rug out from under my feet. To tell you the truth, I'm feeling a bit overwhelmed right now."

Seren hugged me to him just a little tighter and

planted a tender kiss on my cheek. Just that simple show of affection did a lot to calm my racing thoughts. The feel of being cradled in someone's arms really was the best feeling in the world.

"Ask away," my elven suitor urged. "We have the rest of the day to talk and enjoy the ride. Let us see if I can give you something firm to stand on again."

Little did he know that he had already done just that.

CHAPTER SEVEN

To my utter delight, I didn't have to wait long to attend my first elven social gathering. Two days after my elvensteed adventure with Seren, I found out during my now daily Elvish lesson Emily had arranged for me with a couple of the other brides that a gathering was to take place in the main courtyard of the palace tonight.

"What's the occasion?" I had asked Amanda, a twenty year old blonde originally from Canada who had only been living in the elven realm for a little over a year.

"Boredom probably," she had said with a giggle. "There always seems to be at least one party once a moon-cycle. At least they're lots of fun. Great food, beautiful music, and dancing all night. I'm lucky that Beinnon likes to dance and doesn't mind taking me to most of them. Chloe's husband seems to always be too 'busy' whenever the word party is mentioned. Sometimes she and a couple of the other girls will go with Emily, but things like this are always a lot more fun with a date."

Luckily Seren had stopped to have lunch with me today, and I had tentatively brought up the party, remembering a certain conversation from a dream that had turned out to be a lost memory. After he had assured me that he really didn't mind taking me, he had also warned that Locien would likely be attending with Hilde.

Now, standing inside my closet with Mana, one of my attendants—the idea of which I still couldn't get used to—helping me to pick out an appropriate dress, I began to wonder if going was such a good idea after all. The mistress and the wife at the same party along with the mistress's other lover—God, it sounded like an overdone plot of a cheesy soap opera. I definitely wasn't ready to meet Hilde yet, and when we did meet, I sure as hell didn't want it to be with the whole of the elven court looking on.

Plus, I hadn't seen Locien since the night he and Seren had kissed me goodnight in front of my bedroom door. I was beginning to wonder if I would only see him when he and Seren decided to sleep with me. Seeing him with Hilde would only drive that very likely fact harder into my face.

I sighed and shook myself out of my troubling thoughts. I knew what was what when I had decided to come here. I had no right to whine about it now.

When Seren finally knocked on my bedroom door, I had managed to calm my thoughts enough that I was pretty sure I could successfully hide any lingering misgivings from the observant elf. I hurried to open the door before Mana could get up from her chair.

Standing in the doorway, Seren was the very picture of elven nobility, dressed in robes of shimmering silver and baby blue.

"Ready to go?" he asked after his eyes traveled down the length of me, offering me his arm.

I nodded eagerly as I linked our arms together. "I'm really looking forward to hearing some elven music. I keep hearing how beautiful it is from the other brides."

"We can dance, too, if you like."

"I would, but…"

"But?"

I smiled wryly. "I don't think the type of dancing I'm used to would be appropriate here. I imagine things like the waltz would be more your style here."

"Then I shall teach you," he said. "You should have no trouble learning at least the basic steps to some of our more popular dances tonight."

When we entered the sitting room, I was surprised to see Locien standing alone next to one of the couches. I had figured he and Hilde had already left for the party to avoid any accidental meetings. Had something happened?

"Megan, Hilde would very much like to speak with you for a moment before we all go to tonight's gathering," Locien said before either Seren or I could speak.

I sucked in a sharp breath. That was the absolute last thing I had expected him to say.

"I—" I took a deep breath to steady myself. "Is there a particular reason why she wants to meet *now*?"

Locien nodded. "She is worried about you, I believe."

"Worried? About *me*?" I said incredulously.

I couldn't for the life of me fathom her reasoning. Although still extremely reluctant, my curiosity about her motives was stronger, so I gave my consent against my better judgment.

The woman that appeared in the entrance to the hallway across the room was not at all the image I had formed of Locien's wife. To say that she would have killed it on the fashion runways in Milano would have been the understatement of the millennium. Her golden blonde hair trailed down her back in lush waves over an unfairly narrow waist to brush the backs of her knees, but also framing her narrow face perfectly to highlight her high cheekbones and large, peridot-shaded eyes. The only thing that saved this elven woman from being completely intimidating was the sweet expression on her face.

She slowly made her way over to us, and I stepped away from Seren's side to better receive her. Although I thought it was impossible, her beauty intensified when she smiled at me. I couldn't help but smile back, it was so infectious.

"I apologize for the suddenness of my request," she said, "but I felt this was too important to ignore."

"No apologies needed. I'm glad to meet you," I assured her, feeling the last of my nervousness fade. So far this had not been the awkward meeting I had envisioned.

"I shall be brief as I do not wish to keep you from the festivities," Hilde continued. "Everyone will be watching both of us tonight. Our arrangement has been quite the talk of the court, so of course, every blink, every word, every glance will be scrutinized. There are those who wish for us to make a public spectacle of ourselves, to show the folly of inviting a mistress or even a secondary bride within our household. Any child you will have will be a direct heir to the throne, thus weakening the claim of those families within the House of Elerren farther removed from the main branch than our bloodline. There are those who will pray for our failure to produce an heir and those who will strive to make it so by their own hands. The Royal Wife's own past troubles and the more recent tampering of your mind are proof of that."

Hilde reached over and gently took my hands into both of her own and gave them an affectionate squeeze. "Thus, we must give them no opening in which to strike, especially one that never has and never will exist in the first place. I welcome you, Megan, into our family, and when the time is right, I look forward to us being good friends."

She squeezed my hands one last time before releasing them and turning to take Locien's hand again as he stared at both of us with an unreadable expression.

"Thank you," I replied softly. "I would like that very much."

Looking into Hilde's eyes, seeing the absolute sincerity in them when she had told me that she was glad to welcome me into her family, it was then that I knew that this crazy path I had decided to walk down might just work out great in the end. A world of discovery and extraordinary experiences was before me, and for the first time in my life, I found myself almost giddy when I thought about my future.

I squeezed Seren's arm more tightly. "Come on," I said, flashing him a bright smile. "Let's go dance."

CHAPTER EIGHT

I sat out on the balcony, in all appearances gazing out at the rolling hills as the last light of the sun disappeared below the horizon when my mind was in fact a million miles away from them. Seeing Amanda's second child last night and all the excited chatter about it from my group of human friends today had been a very painful reminder that I was letting both Seren and Locien down even though I was sure neither one would see it that way.

Fifty Years.

I frowned. Yes, it really had been that long since I literally followed Seren and Locien blindly into the elven realm. At that time, I never thought that several decades later, my situation would still be teetering along that same line of uncertainty, that I would still be a "mistress" to the House of Elerren.

More importantly, I never thought that I would remain childless after such a long time. Both brothers had assured me time and time again that it wasn't something I needed to worry about, that a child would eventually come along. However, after the conversation between Seren and Locien I had inadvertently overheard this afternoon when I had unexpectedly returned home early from the little get-together with everyone within the royal suite, I was more than worried about my lack of a pregnancy. I was starting to panic.

They had been gravely discussing the possibility that I was as barren as the elven women. The longest any of the human brides had gone without conceiving had been twenty years.

I had left immediately, not wanting to hear any more of their discussion. I didn't want to hear any talk about going back to the human world to find another human bride candidate. I didn't think either one would kick me to the curb if it did turn out that I would never be able to conceive an elven child, but things in the royal family were never so cut and dry in regards to a member's desires. Would I even be allowed to remain here in the Realm if I would never become the bride of an elf?

I had nothing to go back to in the human realm. My old world would now be as alien to me as the elven realm had been all those years ago. Everyone I once knew would be in their seventies, or quite possibly even dead. There was no way I could ever reintegrate into human society again. That ship had sailed long ago.

I took a deep breath when I realized that my heart had begun to beat much too fast. I needed to calm down. There was no way Seren or Locien would allow that to happen. I was still their mistress, and that alone would be enough to protect me from all the various naysayers and human-haters even if—I swallowed thickly against the very large knot that had suddenly formed in my throat—even if they brought in a second mistress.

And they would. I had no doubt about that. Every time a new birth had been announced, every time I had been with either of them when we had encountered someone with a new baby, I had seen the longing and infinite sadness in their eyes. Hilde's as well. How much longer would she tolerate me sleeping with her husband if nothing would ever come of it? Maybe it was Hilde that I was failing most of all because out of all of us, she was the one that had given up the most in this arrangement.

"I still cannot quite fathom your fascination for these rooms," a voice suddenly said behind me, startling me out of my morose thoughts.

"Sometimes quiet is good," I replied with a shrug, schooling my expression into a more pleasant one as I turned to look at Seren over my shoulder.

One of the servants must have spotted me entering this wing and tattled. I knew they meant well and Seren and Locien's words and commands carried almost as much authority as King Sethian's, but sometimes I wished they would keep certain things behind their teeth. I definitely wasn't ready to face either him or Locien when my thoughts and emotions were still such a mess.

"You looked as though something was troubling you, Megan," Seren remarked, his brow furling in worry.

I cursed inwardly. Just how long had he been standing behind me watching me without me knowing?

And just like that, while frantically searching for a way to answer him that wouldn't be a complete lie, a mad idea sprung forth. It was certainly not a new idea, or even a new desire. It was something I had been thinking about a lot lately but never had any intention of acting upon it.

But now—knowing that Seren had just come from a discussion with Locien about my questionable fertility, that desire was suddenly something I wanted desperately to become a reality. I needed it. I needed something I could hold on to, to remember if all I feared would soon come to pass. If I could have just this one thing, then it would be enough.

I turned fully around to face Seren and grabbed one of his hands.

"Come with me," I said firmly, tugging his hand as I drew him away from the balcony's edge and back through the open balcony doors.

It might have been confusion or simply curiosity, but Seren followed me willingly enough without a word. It wasn't until it became obvious that I was leading him into one of the long-empty bedrooms that I felt him hesitate with a slight tug to our joined hands as we crossed the threshold.

It had been quite a while since I had last hidden away in this room to wallow in my uncertainty back in those early days within this realm, so I was not at all surprised that the room smelled vacant and dusty, the only light coming through the opened door from the flickering light of the oil lamp I had left in the sitting room. These days, hardly anyone, even the servants, came to this wing of the palace and for good reason. This had been the suite of the late queen.

"Megan."

My heart sank painfully. He only used that tone when he knew he was about to disappoint me, the one that always made me feel guilty, and in all these decades, I had never once managed to change what he had already decided. However, tonight I would *not* let my guilt *or* his fortitude stop me. No, not tonight.

I didn't react to his voice at all as I continued to pull his hand behind me, and after another couple of seconds of mild resistance, Seren wordlessly allowed me to continue leading him into the bedroom. I knew better than to think I had won this first battle so easily, but his behavior now was one of the things I loved about Seren. He would always indulge me, hear me out, even if in the end, the answer was no.

Once inside, I didn't release his hand as I turned back to him with a sense of determination. I would not let him win this time. Not with this. I had always sensed that Seren was always much more reserved than he would have liked while we made love along with Locien, so I desperately wanted to know what it was like to truly make love with him without the shadow of one we both loved over us.

I didn't want him to be careful; I didn't want him to be considerate. I wanted him to be free of every inhibition and give me his everything while I did the same.

I was briefly thrown off balance by the utter lack of expression on his face instead of the admonishment I had expected, his entire demeanor as still and cold as an elven statue.

Yet I forced myself to meet his gaze all the same. "Please Seren," I said, deciding in that moment to forgo laying out any sort of argument and just to give it to him straight. "Just this one time, I want to know what it's like to *really* make love with you and you alone. If fate decides to give me to Locien, then I'll accept it just as I promised, but at least then I won't regret not ever being with you like this."

"Megan—you *know* I cannot," Seren replied quietly, his expression still unreadable. "Not even for you."

I erased the distance between us and wrapped my arms tightly around his waist and buried my face into his chest. Although he didn't lift a finger to stop the embrace and his body remained relaxed, he also made to move to embrace me in turn.

"Just this one night," I repeated, my words muffled as I spoke them into the folds of his robes, but the pain and desperation still clear as day.

Even I was surprised to hear the undercurrents of pain in my tone. It shouldn't have been there as I've always been good at lying to myself, if not to others. God, this was *really* a bad time to realize just how deep my feelings ran for the man before me. It would hurt all the more when he inevitably rejected all of my pleas in the end.

Nevertheless, I had to at least *try*. I didn't want

to live with the regret of this particular "what if" should our arrangement end in a worse case scenario of me losing them both.

"I *cannot.*" This time, it seemed his words were laced with a bit of sadness.

"Seren…*please…*"

Although I didn't plan it, tears began brimming in my eyes as my voice cracked on that last word, and once they had appeared, I didn't try to hold them back. However, I also didn't lift my face from his chest, not really wanting him to see me lose control of my emotions like this. I scrunched my eyes closed more tightly as the warm streams of my pain slowly fell down my cheeks and held him more firmly against me. I took comfort in the fact that at least he was allowing me this, and I would stay like this until either my desperation lessened or he pushed me away.

Both our breathing sounded as loud as a roar in the thick silence that had settled over us, but I made no effort to speak again, conveying through the strength of my embrace what I couldn't, even now, bring myself to say aloud.

We stood there for what could have been only the span of a few dozen heartbeats but felt like an elven mark before I felt Seren's lips press a gentle kiss to the top of my head. Then his arms were winding around by body, and I was being lifted up until I was cradled against his chest, bridal-style.

I pulled my face away from his chest and finally looked up at him, momentarily forgetting the tears that still stained my cheeks as I wondered if this was his final answer, that he was about to take me back home. However, the look on his face was far from the sad, apologetic look I had expected. It was an expression I had never seen before, sharp and wary and completely focused on me as though he expected me to do or say something either utterly profound or terrifying.

Then without warning, Seren turned and tumbled us both onto the large bed behind us. I had exactly the length of one sharp gasp to marvel that a cloud of dust had not risen from the coverlet as my back hit the mattress with some force before my gasp was swallowed by a hungry mouth and a thrusting, determined tongue.

I lay frozen for one shocked moment as Seren's weight pressed me deeper into the softness at my back, and he kissed me with more ardor and abandon than he had ever shown me before. But then I was opening my mouth wider to him and sucking on his tongue while also spreading my legs in order to allow him to settle himself completely between them.

He thrust his hips roughly against my groin,

causing the delicate fabric of my underwear to slide delightfully against my clit. A spark of pleasure shot up my spine and forced a surprised moan from deep within my throat. I gripped his waist more tightly between my slightly-raised thighs as he thrust again and slid one of my hands over the silkiness of his robes to grab one of his firm mounds through the material and squeezed appreciatively.

Although both he and Locien had warned me against it, I reached a hand up to card through his hair, only this time I deliberately stroked the point of his ear lightly between my thumb and index finger. Seren jumped so violently that it almost seemed as though he had started to seize, the eyes that looked wildly down at me dilated so completely that they looked completely black in the dim light.

Before I could apologize, his mouth was once again crashing down onto mine while his hands tore at the laces of my bodice, snapping a few before it opened completely. I completely expected him to literally rip my dress from my body in the frenzied state he was in. A huge part of me was thrilled at the idea of the always-in-control Seren handling me so roughly, and I trembled with barely contained excitement when I felt his hands gripping my breasts so forcefully through the thin material still covering them.

That's why it was almost a shock when his hands paused and he rather deliberately drew them away from my chest to fist the coverlet on either side of my body. His frenzied kisses also slowed to a single firm brush of the lips before he raised his head just enough that there were a couple of inches between our lips.

Seren closed his eyes and took a long, shuddering breath. When they reopened, a good bit of their wildness had faded.

"Wait," he said, his voice strained with tension. I shivered as his moist breaths teased over my swollen lips. "Wait until I am deep inside you. *Then* I want you to caress my ears again."

That he would request this of me made my heart clench painfully in my chest with a rush of various emotions. He and Locien had always attended to me during our romps as though their pleasure was something secondary. Seren had *never* asked for anything.

I raised a hand up to his face and cupped his cheek lovingly. "Whatever you want," I said huskily.

He turned and kissed the center of my palm before bending down to brush his lips softly against mine. He then sat up onto his knees, still straddling my waist but his body no longer touching me. He reached down and grasped the hem of my dress. I raised my arms over my head, and it was pulled up and over my head quickly, disappearing over the side of the bed. I raised my hips a bit, and my underwear soon joined my discarded dress over the side.

Naked and still breathing heavily, I raised myself onto my elbows and watched with hooded eyes as my elven lover removed all his various layers of robes in record time until only his breeches remained. I sat up the rest of the way and reached to draw them down his muscled thighs, revealing his very aroused, already leaking manhood. Before I could take that impressive member into my hand, he moved completely off my body and finished pulling his breeches the rest of the way off.

I let myself fall back onto the bed as Seren returned to me. I reached up to his shoulders and pulled him down onto me again, loving the way his skin felt pressed against the whole of me, like a warm sheet of silk. In all the countless times I had slept with Seren and Locien, this was something neither brother had allowed themselves to do—to lay upon me as though I had belonged to only him, alone. This was what I had been missing, this simple form of intimacy, what I had longed for but didn't know how to ask them for.

Seren spent a few long moments kissing me senseless again, the fingers of one hand caressing and pinching one of my nipples while grinding his hips against my groin in slow, sensual circles until my sex began to throb insistently with need. I thrust up against him to increase that delicious friction, my own hand alternating between running my fingers through his hair and running them teasingly down his back and then more firmly over the swell of his buttocks until he shivered in reaction.

Then he was positioning his cock at my entrance, and I moaned in approval and opened my legs wider to give him better access. I arched my back as I felt him fill me completely in one hard thrust, my fingernails digging involuntarily into the soft flesh of his back that had him hissing in mild pain.

Pulling out until only the head of his cock remained within my body, Seren grabbed the backs of my thighs and pushed my legs farther up as he continuously thrust his thick length as deeply as possible into my slick passage with every powerful roll of his hips. I slipped my arms through his to grasp the backs of his shoulders tightly, hugging his chest closer to my own while both my heels rested on the backs of his thighs.

My entire body jolted sharply as we continued to rock against each other, the pressure building within my clit moving towards that white-hot explosion that would soon have me screaming.

"Touch me," Seren murmured into my ear, followed by a playful nip to the shell, reminding me of my promise earlier.

Shuddering at the sensation, I turned my head, deciding in that moment to use my mouth and tongue instead. My tongue darted out and slowly, I began to lick up along the inside contours of the shell of his ear. As before, the affect was immediate. Seren released a moan that sounded as though it was ripped from deep within him while the rest of his body seemed to spasm even as he never lost the hard rhythm of our sensuous dance, the tempo of each hard thrust nearly doubling.

He pressed his ear closer to my mouth in encouragement as I continued to lick and run my lips along the hard outer edges just as thoroughly as I did when it was his cock I was caressing with my mouth.

I was so close to exploding, each of his frenzied thrusts hitting that spot deep within me *just right* that had my nerves singing and me seeing bursts of light behind my closed eyelids. I wanted to make him explode along with me. I raised my hand to the other ear poking invitingly out of his hair, lightly brushing over the delicate and extremely sensitive tip with my fingertips while I moved to suck on the tip of the other.

Seren moaned even louder than before, and I swear I felt his cock swell to an impossible width within me as his thrusts became more erratic and brutal and *fantastic*. A couple more well-placed thrusts and I was soon screaming my ecstasy as a wave of pleasure erupted from my groan and thundered up my spine until I saw white, and *still*, Seren continued to fill me as my inner muscles clenched and convulsed around his member.

Only after I gave one final nip to his ear did my elven lover finally plunge heavily into my tight heat with a groan that was pure satisfaction, and the warmth of his seed flooded my passage. As his cock continued to spasm within me, I moved my lips from his ear and slid them over the skin of his cheek to his slightly parted lips, capturing and sucking on his bottom lip teasingly for a moment before moving on to a more thorough kiss that he enthusiastically reciprocated.

I couldn't stop kissing him, enveloping his body completely with my own as I basked in the feel of his weight pressing me down into the mattress. Experiencing Seren this way was everything I had hoped it would be, satisfying everything I had longed for within the uncertainty of my relationship with my elven suitors. I didn't want it to end even though I knew that we had probably indulged ourselves for longer than we should have. Much longer, and someone would realize that we both were missing, and it wouldn't take a genius to figure out why.

I'd had my wish granted, and now it was time to return to reality, something that was becoming increasingly harder to convince myself needed to be done once my elven lover had decided to start sucking on my breast…

Not that I had tried all that hard.

CHAPTER NINE

The next morning was the first morning I had awoken feeling so utterly alone in a very long time. It wasn't that the space beside me was empty. I was used to that as the only times I had a bedmate were on the nights Seren and Locien joined me for sex. Being the center of an elven brother sandwich several times a moon-cycle had always more than fulfilled my needs for nightly companionship, and both men went out of their way to spend time with me in numerous other activities.

Seren and I had horseback riding to share, and Locien enjoyed just sitting with me out on the balcony or walking in the gardens while he told me various elven stories or even just speaking about something as simple as what he had been doing the previous day. In turn, he eagerly absorbed all the information I could tell him about the human world.

It was a routine we had all fallen into fairly quickly, and I had found, to my surprise, that I was a thousand times happier in my new, fairly simple life than I had been back home. I had never once regretted my decision to come to the elven realm, and I didn't regret making love with Seren the way we did last night.

However, doing so had made it virtually impossible now to be satisfied with a relationship stuck in a seemingly perpetual limbo. It understandably made me want something, want *someone* that I quite possibly might never have.

Getting what you wanted was supposed to be a good thing; I had my memory of one perfect night with the man I loved more than anything in this world. I had honestly thought it would be enough, but lying here feeling a hollowness in my heart that had not been present yesterday made it all too clear that I had ultimately just made things worse for myself.

Even so, I couldn't regret it. There was a price to pay for everything, and it was my own damned fault that I hadn't taken that price into consideration at all. No use whining about it now. I would just continue on like I always did and try to bury this new emptiness I had created.

After all, there was still a decent chance I would get to fill that emptiness in the end.

I sat up, wincing as my entire body felt as achy and sore as though I had just run an uphill marathon yesterday. Still, today was one of the days in the cycle that I usually helped the stable workers groom the elvensteed, and sore or not, I wouldn't miss it for the world. There was something so peaceful about grooming such a beautiful animal, and lord knows I could use a little peace right now, especially since I needed to figure out how best to bring up my pregnancy concerns with both Locien and Seren without letting them know that I had eavesdropped on their conversation yesterday.

Once I had washed up and dressed, I was about to open my bedroom door when I finally noticed the angry voices beyond, male voices, though muffled and distant, could only belong to Seren and Locien as the brothers seldom ever invited anyone into the suite unless it was the royal couple. Concern washed over me. Normally they both would have been in the throne room for the morning court session at this time. Had something happened?

I debated on whether or not to leave the room. They always tried to keep me shielded from the political side of things here at the palace, and I had always been grateful for their efforts. As a mistress, I was already in a pretty precarious position in elven society, and I could only imagine what a mess I would have made of everything had I been allowed to involve myself in all the various intrigues of the courtiers.

From the sound of it, whatever they were discussing had to be pretty serious. I definitely shouldn't interrupt them now. I turned back around, intent on sitting down on my bed to wait them out, but a very clear mention of my name as their voices grew louder had me freezing before I could take more than one step.

I moved back to the door and pressed my ear against it, my heart suddenly in my throat. Had someone...

"If you knew what we were doing, then why didn't you confront us right then and there?" Seren demanded, his voice now as clear as though he was standing right outside my door. "Why trouble His Majesty at all when it was something we should have addressed within our household?"

"What more do I need to know other than my own brother has betrayed me in the worst way possible?" Locien replied tightly, his voice so thick with anger that it was nearly unrecognizable. "I *saw* the way you touched each other, the way you allowed her to caress you in that most intimate of ways! The familiarity of that act alone tells me that it was not the first time!"

"Brother…"

"Say no more!" Locien spat. "We shall all hear both of your excuses before the throne. It is for Sethian to judge you now. Now go wake her."

Silence fell for the space of a couple of breaths before the sound of the front door of the suite slamming shut reverberated in the distance like a clap of thunder. I was pulling open the bedroom door within moments.

Seren stood a few feet from the front door, his shoulders slumped, staring at it as though he hoped Locien would somehow come back. I didn't enter any farther into the room. I had made him look like this—dejected, guilty. I had no right to approach him now.

"The only one who should be punished is me," I said into the heavy silence, "and I will tell His Majesty just that."

He turned to me, his mouth set in a grim line. "This is not your fault."

"Of course it is!" I cried. "*I* was the one that asked you to break the promise that you had made to Locien! I never *once* considered the enormity of what that would mean for you, of what it could do to your relationship if he found out. It was selfish, and I *should* be punished for it. If *anyone* has betrayed anyone here, then it was *me* who betrayed you both!"

Seren crossed the room in record time and grabbed both my shoulders. "Listen to me, Megan," he said sternly. *"This is not your fault.* The only ones to blame here are the ones who created this situation in the first place."

"What do you mean?" I asked with a frown.

"I speak of Locien and me," he replied bluntly. He silenced me with a finger against my lips when I tried to protest. "To even find a woman willing to put up with our impossible demands was, frankly, a miracle, and what do we do with that miracle? We ask of her to live a life that could very well never move forward. I marvel that you have never demanded anything of us before last night."

"Is that why you gave into me," I asked softly. "That you think it was somehow my *due?"*

He smiled prettily at me. "No, I did it because it was *you* that asked it of me, and that is exactly what I shall tell His Majesty and Locien both." He released my shoulders and gently took my face into his hands. "His Majesty has ordered us both to stand before the throne. You must leave the explanations to me."

I shook my head. "But——!"

"You must," he repeated with an air of finality. He leaned down and kissed me softly on the forehead. "It will be all right, Megan. I shall make it so, I promise."

So why did his words suddenly fill me with dread?

CHAPTER TEN

Walking into the throne room after being announced by the herald felt as dire and terrifying as I imagined walking the final path of my execution would feel like. I had to keep reminding myself that it was King Sethian who would be sitting in today's judgment seat, that *Emily* would likely be present also, both people that I had gotten to know so well over the decades that I could truly call them family now. He would, at the very least, consider whatever Seren planned to tell him fairly.

In all the years living within the elven realm, I had never set foot within the throne room. Before now, I had never had a reason to, having never had a child to present to the Court. I expected the chamber to be filled with the disapproving eyes of at least a thousand elven nobles that I would be expected to walk past. That's why I was almost confused when other than the herald who had announced us and the guards at the entrance, the only people in the chamber were the king on his throne shining as brightly as the sun and Locien standing stiffly with his back to us at the foot of the dais.

I walked exactly two steps behind Seren and to his right as was courtly protocol, trying to keep a completely neutral expression on my face. I had worked myself up into quite a ball of tension by the time we finally arrived at the foot of the dais, Seren pausing to stand next to Locien while I remained standing just behind him. Locien never once turned to look at us, never *moved* at all.

I made sure to keep my eyes fixed on Seren's back so that I didn't accidently look directly at the king and sear my eyes away. Even this far away, Sethian's powerful aura pressed down heavily on me. Of all the times for Emily to be absent…but I supposed the king did not want his judgment to be colored by any bias towards me.

"It has been brought to my attention that an important stipulation of the agreement between the Stewards of the House of Elerren and the human mistress to the House of Elerren, Megan Reyes, was violated yesterday by said mistress and Seren of the House of Elerren," King Sethian announced formally. "As this matter involves the Royal House, I, alone, shall hear all testimony. Seren, step forward."

I watched anxiously as he stepped up onto the first step of the dais and bowed deeply to the king, keeping his head angled down after he had straightened.

"The agreement between you and your brother was one where you would each always have equal opportunity to father a child," Sethian continued. "By coupling with your mistress without the presence of Locien, you have indeed broken trust with him. As I am truly baffled that you, of all men, would do this terrible thing, I would hear your reasons now."

"I would like to make one point clear before I answer," Seren said firmly. "Megan should bear none of the blame for what transpired last night."

"Seren!" I protested loudly.

"Megan—we spoke about this—"

"*No*! I won't be quiet! And I especially won't let you take any of the blame when this whole mess is *completely* my fault!"

I walked over to Locien and grabbed onto the loose sleeve of his arm determinately. Even then, he still wouldn't look at me, but the fact that he hadn't wrenched his arm away gave me hope.

"Locien, what happened last night was the result of my own selfishness." I took a deep breath. I had to do this. "I love you both, but I love Seren more," I confessed. "However, I made a promise—to you, to His Majesty, to the House of Elerren, itself, and never for one moment did I consider going back on my word, even when my feelings for Seren developed into something deeper. Then yesterday, I overheard you two talking, wondering if maybe I was just as barren as the elven women. After fifty years of nothing, I don't blame you. I got scared that the House elders would decide to send me back to the human realm, that they would pressure you both to find another mistress because it was possible that I would never be able to get pregnant.

"So I begged Seren to give me this one night, one night to know what it was like to make love to only him, and afterwards, I would accept whatever fate decided without at least that one regret. And Seren, being the kind soul that he is, was unable to refuse me."

I released my death-hold on Locien's sleeve then turned towards the king and knelt down before him with my head bent in supplication. "I knew the consequences when I asked him to break this one rule. I'll accept whatever punishment Your Majesty decides to give me without protest."

"But *I* shall not," Seren cut in, joining me on his knees in front of the king. "I am not so good as that.

In that moment, when she confessed how deep her love for me truly ran, I would have forever given up my chance to have a child just to grant her any one wish." He looked over at me, and his smile was the most beautiful thing I had ever seen. "I love her."

Seren then turned to Locien, who was looking at both of us with an utterly unreadable expression. "That's why, brother, in order to spare her from punishment, I shall accept all responsibility and withdraw my claim for the right to continue our family line. You see, despite what you may think of me now, I love you just as much as her and want to spare you any further pain, as well."

I looked back at Seren and smiled even though inside, my heart was breaking. To have his love then be denied it all in the same declaration was as painful as a knife to the heart. However, I couldn't be selfish anymore. I'd had my one night, and now I would accept the price just as I had said.

I looked over at Locien and smiled at him, too. If the king proclaimed that I would marry Locien tonight, I would be fine with that because I knew he would be just as a devoted husband as Seren.

The elven brothers really were too good for a girl like me.

"Megan Reyes, do you swear before your king that all you have spoken is true?" King Sethian demanded.

"I swear it," I replied firmly before bowing my head to him.

"I cannot make an exception even for you, Seren," King Sethian said, turning his attention back to Seren. "Once an exception is made for one, then all will demand it. It was difficult enough to get the noble families to accept the special permission I granted that allowed Megan to come to the Realm as a mistress rather than a bride. It was only your standing within the House of Elerren that allowed this special circumstance.

"Thus, here is my final judgment. The initial agreement will stand. However, to avoid any future misunderstandings and temptations, Megan will be moved from your household today to quarters within my own to serve as a lady-in-waiting to the Royal Wife, Emily, up until the time a child is conceived. You both will only be allowed visitation during her fertile days." His eyes flickered back over to me briefly before moving on to settle on Locien. "To settle your grievance, Locien, you alone will be allowed visitation this moon-cycle."

I saw Locien glance at Seren before nodding his head out of the corner of my eye. That simple gesture gave me a measure of hope. Maybe I hadn't broken things between the brothers as badly as I had feared.

Not that it made my guilt any less. The king really had been much too lenient as far as punishments went.

I deserved worse.

CHAPTER ELEVEN

Like some sort of bad *déjà vu*, voices sounded outside my door, at first muffled, then I recognized Emily's as they neared, and—no, it couldn't be—but I would recognize that voice anywhere. I shot up from where I had been lying prone on my bed, staring miserably at the ceiling and calling myself every name in the book. Just what the hell did he think he was doing coming here *now*?

"This is something she definitely needs to hear firsthand," I heard Emily say gravely.

A knock sounded before I could even jump to my feet. "It's Emily. You have some very important visitors."

I was at the door and turning the knob in two seconds flat. The tone of her voice, alone, had made my anxiety shoot through the roof, but that was nothing compared to the shock I received when I realized exactly who was standing directly behind her. Stupidly, I felt tears begin to well up in my eyes. Seren and Locien were here—together—and not staring daggers at each other or even refusing to look at each other as it had been in the throne room. In fact, the two brothers wore the exact same dour expression, uncannily so.

I stepped aside wordlessly and gestured for everyone to come in. It was only then that I noticed Teyan was among them. I couldn't for the life of me even hazard a guess as to why this particular cousin was here.

"Are you sure the king won't be pissed that you let Seren and Locien in here to see me?" I asked Emily worriedly as I sat down next to her on the bed. All three men had opted to stand by the door.

"After he hears what they just told me, me ignoring his decree this one time will be the least of his concerns," she assured me.

"Did something happen to one of the human brides?" I asked anxiously.

Is that why Emily had allowed Seren and Locien to come to my room? Did she think I would need their protection? Thoughts of all the horror stories I had heard of Emily's various assassination attempts surfaced in my mind.

"Yes," Seren said, immediately drawing my attention. I was taken aback at the amount of fury that swirled in his eyes. "Only that bride was *you*."

"Huh?" I said intellectually. I looked from Seren to Locien in utter bewilderment. "But—I'm not hurt at all!"

"Unfortunately, you were hurt far greater than you realize," Emily interjected, her voice tinged with outrage.

"Perhaps I should take over the explanation from here," Teyan said. His expression was strange, something like sadness mixed with another element that I just couldn't put my finger on. "I am ashamed to say that my father has performed a grave injustice to not only you, milady, but also to the stewards of our House."

I blinked at him in surprised. His father? I couldn't remember having any contact with him at all anytime recently and said as much.

Teyan shook his head. "The initial incident goes back much farther, to before Seren and Locien even brought you into the Realm."

"But—the only *Sidhe* I was in contact with back then were Seren and Locien. I don't—" I gasped, the answer finally dawning on me. "My memories! He was the elf that tampered with my mind all those years ago!"

How long had the brothers searched for answers and had come up empty-handed time and time again before I had truly believed that the culprit would remain hidden forever? I guess now, the most important question was, "But why?"

"After nearly twenty years of searching, it had become apparent that Seren and Locien would not find their potential bride with any speed, if at all. I, too, had petitioned the king for the chance to continue my family line and had finally been granted permission to seek my bride in a year's time. It is at this point that my father's perfidy comes into play.

"The next stewardship of our house would naturally fall to the sons of either Locien or Seren, but should the need arise before an heir is born, the title would pass to one of the lesser branches of the family, ideally one who has already produced a child."

"I see," I said dryly. "Your father wanted that title passed on to your family. Maybe even *he* would live to see the title, himself."

Teyan grimaced. "He has never been satisfied with our family's lot. To be so near the throne and yet so far away. That is why he set his sights on the power that *was* obtainable."

"I must have been a nasty surprise. Did he confess all this to you?" I asked.

Teyan snorted. "My father would sooner confess

to wanting to assassinate the king than confide anything to me. I suppose I am just not ambitious enough, and he see that as a weakness he dare not chance with his secrets."

"And what secrets he has," Seren said in disgust. "No, Megan, he was overheard confessing to one of his co-conspirators."

I nodded. "Well, at least he didn't do anything worse to me. I imagine there are easier ways of getting rid of potential roadblocks."

I saw Emily wince in my peripheral and instantly regretted my flippant words. Not too long ago, the Royal Wife had been labeled as such by the elven queen.

"Unfortunately, our cousin Galanir is guilty of much worse," Seren told me angrily. I looked over at him and saw that same anger reflected in Locien's eyes when my gaze shifted over to him as well.

"My father has a mistress," Teyan explained, "a servant that works in the kitchens. He may have been using her to slip a certain herb into your food."

My eyes widened. "Are you trying to tell me that he's been poisoning me!"

"No, not poison," Seren said through gritted teeth. "It is an herb which the anti-human factions within our people discovered caused temporary sterility in humans. It is completely undetectable by our healers once ingested."

"He's been slipping me *birth control*!" I exclaimed in disbelief.

"That is what I fear," Teyan replied solemnly.

That son-of-a-bitch…for fifty years I've had to watch Seren, Locien, and Hilde's disappointment at my inability to get pregnant. To find out all that pain could have been avoided made me absolutely livid with anger.

"If that's true, then Galanir's been playing the long game with all the patience of an immortal," Emily said. "Another couple of decades and Seren and Locien may have started believing that *they* were sterile. From that point, it would have been relatively easy to convince the House elders that the next heir should be his own son, especially since you have a son of your own now, Teyan."

"It upsets me greatly that for all this time, my father had been using my own desire for a family in his quest for political gain."

"Me as well," Locien said.

I turned to him questionably. "How so?"

He closed his eyes, but not before I saw a flash of guilt. "One of Galanir's servants saw both you and Seren enter the abandoned wing last night. It was he who directed me to you."

Seren rested his hand lightly on Locien's shoulder. "You have no blame in any of this, brother," Seren said softly.

Locien opened his eyes and looked at Seren with an unreadable expression. However, he didn't say anything else.

"I only overheard them speaking because my father was talking in a loud, angry voice," Teyan was saying, capturing my attention once again. I had been so focused on watching the interaction between Seren and Locien that I hadn't even realized that the other elf had started talking again. "Apparently, he was not at all pleased with His Majesty's ruling regarding you three this morning."

I winced. I didn't think anyone else had heard about the nature of our hearing this morning. I wondered who else knew.

"So what do we do now?" I asked Seren. Maybe I should go see a healer just to be on the safe side.

"We inform the king and keep a sharp eye on Galanir. Without any direct proof and short of a mind extraction, we cannot level a charge. If he is in fact tampering with your food, Megan, then he may see a dungeon cell sooner rather than later."

"I shall keep a closer eye on him as well," Teyan promised. "If he has had dealings with some of the anti-human groups, then Megan may not be the only human bride being fed the herb. There remain a few brides who have not yet conceived. To deny those families a child is a travesty that must not go unpunished, even if it is my own father."

It was only after everyone had left that I realized that after telling me about Galanir's role in snitching on Seren and me, Locien hadn't said another word.

CHAPTER TWELVE

A few nights later, after bidding goodnight to Emily and her ladies-in-waiting, I returned to find a surprise, though not unwelcomed, visitor in my new bedroom within the royal suite. He had been on my mind quite a bit. His subdued demeanor the last time I had seen him had worried me quite a lot. I wondered if he and Seren had talked more. I hoped that Seren did not make any excuses for me if they did.

Even if he had not been sitting bare-chested on my bed, I would have known exactly why he had come.

I walked over to the bed and climbed onto it, moving on my knees towards his visibly stiff back. I didn't think it was possible, but his body seemed to stiffen even more when I wrapped my arms around his chest from behind.

Locien didn't try to move out of my embrace; he didn't say a word. We stayed that way in that silent, tense embrace for what felt like an eternity. I could tell he was suffering, no doubt agonizing over Seren's and my mutual confessions before the king as well as the treachery Teyan had revealed to all of us a few days ago, and I had no idea how to fix it, how to ease that suffering. No one deserved that kind of guilt, least of all Locien.

In that painful moment, all I could do was hold onto him like this, to silently acknowledge my own very real and deserved guilt in this whole mess, and hopefully he would understand that.

"I should have known," Locien said abruptly into the silence. "It was only inevitable."

"What was?" I asked quietly.

"That you would fall for each other."

His words hung in the air like a thousand weights bearing down onto my shoulders. I hung my head and pressed my forehead lightly between his bare shoulder blades.

"I was asking for too much," he continued, his voice equally as quiet, "For you, for Hilde to accept that neither one of you would ever lay claim to the whole of me. Whereas both you and Seren gave your everything to each other from the very beginning.

No—not just Seren. You gave your all to *me*, as well."

I lifted my head sharply. "*You* did nothing wrong," I said firmly. "You both made it very clear back when you were courting me exactly what I was getting myself into. Truthfully, I never expected to favor one of you over the other, you were both so attentive and charming in your own ways, nor did I expect *fifty* years to pass without me getting pregnant. I naively thought fate would take care of that possible hiccup before it ever became a problem. As I told the king before, this whole mess was the result of *my* selfishness. I pushed Seren into a corner where it was impossible for him to say no.

"But I swear to you, Locien, I never meant for it to go any further than that one night. I just wanted to know what he would be like uninhibited. If there was any betrayal that night, then it was solely mine—to you both. I damaged something that should have never even been touched. For that, I am more sorry than I can ever put into words."

When he remained silent, I bent down and kissed him affectionately on the cheek. "We put our lives into the hands of fate from the start, and I see no reason that should change now. I really am okay with it, Locien, so if you're still okay with someone like me having your children, then let's go to bed."

"I should walk away," he said softly. He turned

to look at me over his shoulder, and I was dismayed to find that I couldn't read his expression at all. "If I did not want a child so badly…"

I nodded solemnly in sudden understanding, but at the same time, I felt even guiltier. He was still trying to apologize to me for not being able to allow Seren and me to be together despite knowing how deep our feelings for each other ran, trying to apologize for wanting a child more than his own brother's happiness even when there was a very big chance he may never have that child he and Hilde so desperately wanted.

Why—*why* did the elves have to make everything so complicated? If only they both would've been allowed to take a human bride…

However, as soon as that thought popped into my mind, I knew my anger and frustration was misplaced. There *were* very good reasons to limit the amount of human women allowed into the elven realm—at least the reasons King Sethian had given us. Once again, this was simply my own selfishness rearing its ugly head, and that selfishness had very nearly given Seren and Locien's enemies the very thing that could have not only unseated them from power, but also ultimately destroyed any chance of them having a child. If the elven king had not been so kind and understanding…

All told, both Locien and Seren had been waiting for nearly seventy years since they had begun their search for a bride to become a father and no doubt centuries before even that. The only thing I *should* have hoped for at this point was to have the ability to give one of them that child because it would be particularly cruel for them after yearning for so long to find that, no, it hadn't been the birth control that had been slipped into my food by the biggest asshole in the universe, but that I had been infertile all along.

Of course, I didn't let any of those conflicting thoughts and emotions show in my expression as I smiled at Locien before I moved away to begin unlacing my bodice. I was more relieved than I wanted to admit when Locien turned and grasped the hem of my dress, lifting it up my body and over my head once all the laces had been undone. Had he ultimately decided to reject me despite everything he had just said, then I would have feared that his relationship with Seren would have been broken forever.

I was determined to keep my promise to him, no matter how much pain that promise may end up causing me in the future. After all, that pain had been inevitable from the start. I had just been too naïve and stupid to see it, unlike my two suitors.

Locien allowed me to help him out of his pants, but although this was something I had done countless times, the air about us was like it was the first time, cautious and deliberate, almost as though we were strangers again rather than the light and carefree manner of all the times before I had screwed everything up. That's why it was actually a shock when he suddenly pulled me closer with a firm press of his hand against the back of my head and crushed his lips against mine. I honestly had not thought that he would ever kiss me again.

I opened my mouth to his probing tongue and closed my eyes out of instinct, hastily grabbing onto his shoulders to steady myself. He slipped his other arm around my waist and pulled me closer still, until I had risen up onto my knees and my bare breasts were pressed flush against his chest. I moved my hands from his shoulders to wrap my arms around his neck and tilted my head to the right in order to allow him better, deeper access to my mouth.

Although his initial kiss had been a little rough, the following kisses had slowed, gentled. They were more affectionate caress rather than passionate, the silkiness of his lips rubbing against and sucking on my mouth feeling pleasant and soothing. It was completely opposite of the last kisses I had shared with Seren where we had practically devoured each other.

Despite everything, the affection Locien and I had shared for one another was still present, and I once again found myself relieved. I may not love Locien as deeply as I loved Seren, but I *did* love him. Had my actions with Seren a few nights ago destroyed that affection between us permanently and I ended up becoming pregnant with Locien's child, it would have been difficult for both of us to be trapped in that kind of loveless marriage, especially knowing that both of us loved someone else.

Maybe I hadn't screwed everything up as badly as I had first thought. Maybe I *could* fix what I had broken. Because no matter who ended up being the father of my child, it had always been my hope that Seren, Locien, and Hilde would all become an important part of my child's life.

Yes, I was definitely too naïve for my own good.

I reached down to encircle his already hardening cock in my hand, giving it a playful squeeze before sliding my hand up and down along its entire length, my thumb moving teasingly over the head with every upward stroke. He made a small noise low in his throat, and his arm around me abruptly tightened.

A few moments later, it was my turn to gasp as one of his hands made its way down my belly to the throbbing, moist center of my sex and began to slowly rub circles over the sensitive nub with a couple of his fingers. I pulled my lips away from his and moved to suck on his neck, the movements of my hand on his member speeding up in response to my rising excitement.

Once I was sufficiently wet and trembling, Locien gently moved my hand away from his cock and sat back onto his haunches. He then grabbed both my buttocks and wordlessly urged me to climb onto his lap. I moved forward to straddle him, reaching back to palm his cock again in order to position it at my opening.

I shivered as I slowly sank down onto him, both from the sensation of being filled and the intense way he was studying my face as I did it. Was he looking for hints of my true feelings while my mind was fuzzy with pleasure? Did he think I was just humoring him, that I had been lying when I had said I cared for him, in order to protect Seren? The thought made my heart ache, but I had no one but myself to blame.

Why did I always have to do these kinds of stupid things? Here I was, having lived for over seventy years, and it seemed I was no wiser than I had been as a twenty-something.

I brutally forced all of that from my mind, determined to give the man in my arms my full attention. I would have plenty of time later to curse my stupidity when I was alone.

I leaned forward and kissed him tenderly on his lips before I wrapped my arms tightly around his shoulders and back and began to rock my hips in earnest. His fingers gripped my buttocks more tightly as he continued to watch me with that same, penetrating gaze. I met his gaze squarely, opening myself to him completely in all ways even as my breathing began to accelerate along with the mounting pressure within my groin.

My inner walls clenched his member more tightly as my pace increased, and I was rewarded with a flash of pleasure in his eyes and a hitch in his breath. I was glad, glad that Locien was finding pleasure in our coupling even while he was still so obviously conflicted about everything.

On the verge of climax, I bent to kiss him again, this time a lot more aggressively as my excitement crested and then exploded into orgasm. Locien pulled me closer against him for a moment as I rode out the waves of my climax, before gently tumbling me onto my back once my hips had slowed. I wrapped my still-trembling legs around his thighs as he began to thrust into me with quick, powerful strokes, our tongues tangling just as frantically.

With one final, heavy thrust, he groaned into my mouth as his seed erupted within me, and I swallowed that sound eagerly. His hips immediately picked up again for a few more rapid, shallow thrusts until all of his seed was spent.

Rather than collapse on top of me, he let himself fall onto his side, withdrawing his cock from my body in the process but also pulling me to lie against him. I tangled our legs together and wrapped my arms around him.

I lay still and silent wrapped up in the warmth of his body, listening to his breathing and the rapid beating of his heart as they both gradually evened out. There was so much I still wanted to say to him, but I was loath to break the peaceful silence that had settled over us.

"I'm sorry."

Locien's unexpected words seemed to echo in the stillness. Stricken, I could only squeeze him tighter. Maybe this was a wound that would never heal.

It was something that would haunt me for nearly a year.

CHAPTER THIRTEEN

When Seren suddenly stopped dead in his tracks at my bedroom door, a look of absolute disbelief on his face, I had to stop myself from suddenly turning around to see what type of monster had managed to sneak up behind me. Then before I could blink, he was hugging me, then twirling me around, making me think that maybe he had suddenly gone off the deep end.

It didn't help that about two seconds later, Locien was prying Seren off me and glaring fit to kill. "What in the name of the higher powers do you think you are doing?" Locien hissed.

"I could ask you the same thing, brother," Seren shot back, matching the older elf glare for glare.

My heart sank. Were they fighting again? Although it had taken a few moon-cycles, Seren and

Locien had managed to talk out their differences, especially after that whole brouhaha involving Galanir that had occurred only a moon-cycle after Teyan had ratted out his father.

In an effort to catch their treacherous cousin in the act, Seren and Locien had arranged to have Galanir's mistress watched like a hawk by several of the kitchen workers, and a moon-cycle later, their efforts had been rewarded when one of the workers witnessed the mistress adding an unknown powder to my breakfast one morning. The suspect food was immediately sent to the healers, who were able to confirm that the powder was indeed the "contraceptive herb."

Threatened with a mind extraction, she easily gave up her lover, who when threatened with the same, spilled the beans on what not only he, but several members of an anti-human group had been up to. Having executed the *queen* by mind extraction, Galanir had known better than to believe that King Sethian had been bluffing.

It seemed the goal of the anti-human brigade was to prevent *all* pregnancies, and I'd had the dubious honor of being the first human bride that they had seriously tested it on. They had waited patiently for fifty years to see if I would indeed remain childless and had just begun giving the herb to many of the brides when their scheme had been revealed.

I shook myself out of my thoughts. Now was not the time to replay that whole mess.

"First you're giddy, and now you look ready to spit nails. What exactly have you two been smoking?" I asked in utter bewilderment.

"Of *course* I'm giddy," Seren replied, his glare melting into a grin that threatened to split his face in half as he looked back at me.

When I continued to stare at him as though he had suddenly grown an extra head, his expression changed yet again, but this time to surprise. "You have no idea, do you?"

"About what?" I asked, throwing up my hands in exasperation. I was beginning to wonder if I was still asleep and this was all just some bizarre dream.

Seren reached out a hand and pressed it gently against my belly. "That our child currently lies within you."

I stilled completely, certain that I had heard him wrong. "W-What?"

"Our child," Seren repeated. "I can hear our child's soul."

"That is impossible."

The harsh tone of those words had me auto-matically looking at Locien even as my mind was on the verge of imploding. I was—*pregnant?* I didn't feel pregnant. I didn't feel different at all!

However, Locien wasn't looking at me but at Seren, and that's when I saw it. Within a split-second it had come and gone, but it was there again—the suspicion, the distrust, but what was worse was that flash of betrayal. Would he *ever* be able to trust Seren as completely as he once did?

"It's true," Seren said gently, his expression suddenly filled with understanding and sympathy.

"It cannot be your child," Locien insisted, "else I would not be able to hear the child's soul as clearly as though it were shouting into my ear!"

This time it was Seren's eyes that narrowed in suspicion. "I would not lie about something so momentous."

Locien rushed forward and grabbed Seren by the front of his robes. "That it is such a momentous occasion is the very reason why you would!" he snarled.

When it became apparent that the situation was about to devolve into blows, I rushed over to the bickering elves and yanked hard on Locien's arm. "Stop!" I cried. "Neither one of you are thinking clearly at all! If you're both hearing the baby's soul, then wouldn't a better explanation be that it's because I'm carrying *twins* than the two of you are suddenly liars? I've heard of dual fathers happening before with fraternal twins in the human world."

"Twins are extremely rare among the *Sidhe*," Locien said, sounding dubious, "so rare, in fact, that there are currently only three pairs within the Realm."

"Well, according to my late grandmother, they aren't rare in *my* family," I retorted.

In the back of my mind, I marveled at how calmly I had accepted my impending motherhood when fifty years ago it would have been the end of the world for me. It was a good thing, too, because right now it didn't look as though either brother was ready to back down.

"I shall send for Yara," Seren announced, shooting Locien a challenging look. "Let us end this now."

I have to admit, I was relieved. Yara was the healer I had seen after finding out about the contraceptive herbs in my food. Her no-nonsense attitude was exactly what was needed here.

While Seren went off to find a servant, Locien urged me to lie down on the bed. While he fussed over me, I decided I had to at least try to smooth things out again.

"Locien, you know as well as I do that Seren would never lie about something this important," I said quietly. "I hate seeing you two so much at odds with each other. I hate that it was me that caused the rift to begin with. You two are brothers. You're about to become *fathers*. I don't want to think that the hurt I stupidly caused is something that will never heal."

"It will, I think," Locien replied after a long moment of silence. "Perhaps when I can forgive myself." He brushed a hand lovingly across my stomach. "Of course, now when things should have been simpler, we all had to go and muddy the waters again."

"I don't think it has to be so complicated. Maybe some higher power somewhere took pity on us and made this miracle happen, because I truly believe that *both* your children are now growing inside me."

"Fate, itself, perhaps?" Locien ventured with a smile. "Even so, a complication still remains. You must still become a wife to one of us in order to give legitimacy to the heir."

"Don't you elves have adoption?" I asked in exasperation. "We'll all be living in the same household anyway, so I don't see why you and Hilde can't claim our child in that way even if I'll be doing the majority of the mothering. Then I'll be free to marry Seren, and you won't feel so awful about not giving your all to your wife or taking a potential wife from your brother. Don't try to deny it. Plus, you'll have *two* heirs to continue your bloodline. A win-win all around."

"His Majesty would have to approve it," Locien

said slowly, something like hope rising in his eyes for the first time in a long time.

I snorted. "Do you really think he would say no? I think at this point he's as frustrated with the tension between you two as the rest of us."

Before Locien could answer, Seren returned. "It's good that you are resting," he said, smiling in approval.

"I really do hope that you two don't plan on nagging me this much for my entire pregnancy," I said with a sigh. Then I grinned. "So Locien, do you want to tell Seren all about my brilliant plan or should I?" I asked innocently.

EPILOGUE

Looking at Seren and Locien as they cradled our sons in their arms, I couldn't help but feel a bit of tightness behind my eyes as I was suddenly overwhelmed with a flood of various emotions. This was definitely a scene I had never in a million years thought was possible, especially considering the year of heartache we had all endured before a pregnancy, of all things, had changed everything for the better.

Blond like their fathers, I had never seen anything more adorable than their cute little elf ears poking out from swirls of hair finer than silk. Of course, I was terribly biased.

From my perch on the bed, I quietly observed Locien and Hilde as the latter cooed over the baby with so much joy in her eyes that had I not already been on the brink of tears, it would have definitely brought me to tears. Not surprisingly, all the awk-wardness between us had disappeared once my mar-riage to Seren had become official. I was no longer her husband's mistress but now an official bride of the House of Elerren and her sister-in-law, and no one was happier about that fact than I was even though deep down, I would always miss the intimacy I had shared with Locien.

The birth of the twins had also done a lot to mend the relationship between Seren and Locien. Most of Locien's hurt had stemmed from his own guilt, and now that the potential for another betrayal no longer existed, it was as though the first had never occurred in the first place. The stiffness in Locien's demeanor whenever he was near Seren that had sprung up after the night he had spied us making love in the queen's old suite had entirely disappeared.

Seren had also lost his air of sadness, and I was relieved to see the happy-go-lucky elf that I had fallen in love with return. Perhaps out of the three of us, I had been the one who hadn't been able to es-cape their guilt completely. I still caught myself star-ing at the brothers on occasion with a kind of melan-cholia that I could not shake for marks afterwards, remembering what I had so very nearly destroyed and terrified that I might somehow do it again some-day.

However, those episodes of brief despair were happening less and less these days, and now that I had two beautiful boys to look forward to raising, I knew the day would come when that dark year of my life would become a distant memory if not forgotten altogether.

After all, I had eons of time to enjoy with my family, and for the first time since I had come to the elven realm, the thought of all those years was not daunting at all.

ABOUT THE AUTHOR

Cristina Rayne lives in West Texas with her crazy cat and about a dozen bookcases full of fantasy worlds and steamy romances. She has a degree in Computer Science which totally qualifies her to write romances. As Fantasy is her first love, she feels if she can inject a little love into the fantastical, along with a few steamy scenes, then all the better. To learn more about upcoming releases or just to chat, visit her blog at http://CristinaRayneAuthor.blogspot.com